SIR ARTHUR CONAN DOYLE

The Mysterious Adventures of Sherlock Holmes

D0062628

PUFFIN BOOKS

PUFFIN BOOKS

Published by the Penguin Group
Penguin Books Ltd, 80 Strand, London WC2R 0RL, England
Penguin Putnam Inc., 375 Hudson Street, New York, New York 10014, USA
Penguin Books Australia Ltd, 250 Camberwell Road, Camberwell, Victoria 3124, Australia
Penguin Books Canada Ltd, 10 Alcorn Avenue, Toronto, Ontario, Canada M4V 3B2
Penguin Books India (P) Ltd, 11 Community Centre, Panchsheel Park, New Delhi – 110 017, India
Penguin Books (NZ) Ltd, Cnr Rosedale and Airborne Roads, Albany, Auckland, New Zealand
Penguin Books (South Africa) (Pty) Ltd, 24 Sturdee Avenue, Rosebank 2196, South Africa

Penguin Books Ltd, Registered Offices: 80 Strand, London WC2R 0RL, England

www.penguin.com

This selection published in Puffin Books 1995
19

'The Greek Interpreter', 'The *Gloria Scott*', 'The Resident Patient' and 'The
Crooked Man' first published in *The Memoirs of Sherlock Holmes*, 1894; 'The
Boscombe Valley Mystery', 'The Noble Bachelor' and 'The Five Orange Pips' first
published in *The Adventures of Sherlock Holmes, 1892*; 'The Three Students', first
published in *The Return of Sherlock Holmes*, 1905.

Filmset by Datix International Ltd, Bungay, Suffolk
Printed in England by Clays Ltd, St Ives plc
Set in 12/15 pt Monophoto Plantin

PUFFIN CLASSICS

The Mysterious Adventures of Sherlock Holmes

Arthur Conan Doyle (1859–1930) studied medicine in his native Edinburgh, graduated in 1881 and set up practice as an oculist. Patients turned out to be few and far between, however, and he turned to writing instead. The most important contribution his medical studies made to his future was that he met Joseph Bell, an Edinburgh surgeon who had a hobby of deducing people's characters from minor details of their appearance. Bell became the model for the most famous literary detective in the world – Sherlock Holmes, who was introduced in 1887 in *A Study in Scarlet*.

Sherlock Holmes was the first scientific detective, who solved cases by deduction rather than because the criminal made a mistake. Conan Doyle thus created the modern detective novel. But Holmes is not just a famous detective – he is probably the best known character in English literature. The tall, angular, pipe-smoking detective, with his deer-stalker hat, is instantly recognizable by everyone; and he had a perfect foil in the plodding Dr Watson. Holmes is so famous that tourists still flock to 221B Baker Street in London, where the fictional detective resided.

Conan Doyle wrote well-received novels in other genres too, and felt at times imprisoned by the success of Holmes. He once killed him off, but then had to revive him by popular demand. Holmes figures in several full-length books, but Conan Doyle found short stories to be the best medium and wrote some fifty of these for the prestigious *Strand Magazine* from 1891 onwards.

Arthur Conan Doyle was knighted in 1902 for his public and published defence of the British cause in the Boer War. After the death of his son in the First World War, he devoted the rest of his life to spiritualism, on which he wrote several books and lectured all around the world.

Some other Puffin Classics to enjoy

THE HOUND OF THE BASKERVILLES
THE GREAT ADVENTURES OF SHERLOCK HOLMES
THE EXTRAORDINARY CASES OF SHERLOCK HOLMES
THE LOST WORLD
Sir Arthur Conan Doyle

Contents

THE GREEK INTERPRETER

During my long and intimate acquaintance with Mr Sherlock Holmes I had never heard him refer to his relations, and hardly ever to his own early life. This reticence upon his part had increased the somewhat inhuman effect which he produced upon me, until sometimes I found myself regarding him as an isolated phenomenon, a brain without a heart, as deficient in human sympathy as he was pre-eminent in intelligence. His aversion to women, and his disinclination to form new friendships, were both typical of his unemotional character, but not more so than his complete suppression of every reference to his own people. I had come to believe that he was an orphan with no relatives living, but one day, to my very great surprise, he began to talk to me about his brother.

It was after tea on a summer evening, and the conversation, which had roamed in a desultory, spasmodic fashion from golf clubs to the causes of the change in the obliquity of the ecliptic, came round at last to the question of atavism and hereditary aptitudes. The point under discussion was how far any singular gift in an individual was due to his ancestry, and how far to his own early training.

'In your own case,' said I, 'from all that you have told me it seems obvious that your faculty of observation and your peculiar facility for deduction are due to your own systematic training.'

'To some extent,' he answered thoughtfully. 'My ancestors were country squires, who appear to have led much the same life as is natural to their class. But, none the less, my turn that way is in my veins, and may have come with my grand-mother, who was the sister of Vernet, the French artist. Art in the blood is liable to take the strangest forms.'

'But how do you know that it is hereditary?'

'Because my brother Mycroft possesses it in a larger degree than I do.'

This was news to me, indeed. If there were another man with such singular powers in England, how was it that neither police nor public had heard of him? I put the question, with a hint that it was my companion's modesty which made him acknowledge his brother as his superior. Holmes laughed at my suggestion.

'My dear Watson,' said he, 'I cannot agree with those who rank modesty among the virtues. To the logician all things should be seen exactly as they are, and to underestimate oneself is as much a departure from truth as to exaggerate one's own powers. When I say, therefore, that Mycroft has

better powers of observation than I, you may take
it that I am speaking the exact and literal truth.'

'Is he your junior?'

'Seven years my senior.'

'How comes it that he is unknown?'

'Oh, he is very well known in his own circle.'

'Where, then?'

'Well, in the Diogenes Club, for example.'

I had never heard of the institution, and my
face must have proclaimed as much, for Sherlock
Holmes pulled out his watch.

'The Diogenes Club is the queerest club in
London, and Mycroft one of the queerest men.
He's always there from a quarter to five till twenty
to eight. It's six now, so if you care for a stroll
this beautiful evening I shall be very happy to
introduce you to two curiosities.'

Five minutes later we were in the street, walking
towards Regent Circus.

'You wonder,' said my companion, 'why it is
that Mycroft does not use his powers for detective
work. He is incapable of it.'

'But I thought you said –!'

'I said that he was my superior in observation
and deduction. If the art of the detective began
and ended in reasoning from an armchair, my
brother would be the greatest criminal agent that
ever lived. But he has no ambition and no energy.
He would not even go out of his way to verify his
own solutions, and would rather be considered
wrong than take the trouble to prove himself right.

Again and again I have taken a problem to him, and have received an explanation which has afterwards proved to be the correct one. And yet he was absolutely incapable of working out the practical points which must be gone into before a case could be laid before a judge or jury.'

'It is not his profession, then?'

'By no means. What is to me a means of livelihood is to him the merest hobby of a dilettante. He has an extraordinary faculty for figures, and audits the books in some of the Government departments. Mycroft lodges in Pall Mall, and he walks round the corner into Whitehall every morning and back every evening. From year's end to year's end he takes no other exercise, and is seen nowhere else, except only in the Diogenes Club, which is just opposite his rooms.'

'I cannot recall the name.'

'Very likely not. There are many men in London, you know, who, some from shyness, some from misanthropy, have no wish for the company of their fellows. Yet they are not averse to comfortable chairs and the latest periodicals. It is for the convenience of these that the Diogenes Club was started, and it now contains the most unsociable and unclubbable men in town. No member is permitted to take the least notice of any other one. Save in the Strangers' Room, no talking is, under any circumstances, permitted, and three offences, if brought to the notice of the committee, render the talker liable to expulsion.

My brother was one of the founders, and I have myself found it a very soothing atmosphere.'

We had reached Pall Mall as we talked, and were walking down it from the St James's end. Sherlock Holmes stopped at a door some little distance from the Carlton, and, cautioning me not to speak, he led the way into the hall. Through the glass panelling I caught a glimpse of a large and luxurious room in which a considerable number of men were sitting about and reading papers, each in his own little nook. Holmes showed me into a small chamber which looked out on to Pall Mall, and then, leaving me for a minute, he came back with a companion who I knew could only be his brother.

Mycroft Holmes was a much larger and stouter man than Sherlock. His body was absolutely corpulent, but his face, though massive, had preserved something of the sharpness of expression which was so remarkable in that of his brother. His eyes, which were of a peculiarly light watery grey, seemed to always retain that far-away, introspective look which I had only observed in Sherlock's when he was exerting his full powers.

'I am glad to meet you, sir,' said he, putting out a broad, flat hand, like the flipper of a seal. 'I hear of Sherlock everywhere since you became his chronicler. By the way, Sherlock, I expected to see you round last week to consult me over that Manor House case. I thought you might be a little out of your depth.'

'No, I solved it,' said my friend, smiling.

'It was Adams, of course?'

'Yes, it was Adams.'

'I was sure of it from the first.' The two sat down together in the bow-window of the club. 'To anyone who wishes to study mankind this is the spot,' said Mycroft. 'Look at the magnificent types! Look at these two men who are coming towards us, for example.'

'The billiard-marker and the other?'

'Precisely. What do you make of the other?'

The two men had stopped opposite the window. Some chalk marks over the waistcoat pocket were the only signs of billiards which I could see in one of them. The other was a very small, dark fellow, with his hat pushed back and several packages under his arm.

'An old soldier, I perceive,' said Sherlock.

'And very recently discharged,' remarked the brother.

'Served in India, I see.'

'And a non-commissioned officer.'

'Royal Artillery, I fancy,' said Sherlock.

'And a widower.'

'But with a child.'

'Children, my dear boy, children.'

'Come,' said I, laughing, 'this is a little too much.'

'Surely,' answered Holmes, 'it is not hard to say that a man with that bearing, expression of authority, and sun-baked skin is a soldier, is more than a private, and is not long from India.'

'That he has not left the service long is shown by his still wearing his "ammunition boots", as they are called,' observed Mycroft.

'He has not the cavalry stride, yet he wore his hat on one side, as is shown by the lighter skin on that side of his brow. His weight is against his being a sapper. He is in the artillery.'

'Then, of course, his complete mourning shows that he has lost someone very dear. The fact that he is doing his own shopping looks as though it were his wife. He has been buying things for children, you perceive. There is a rattle, which shows that one of them is very young. The wife probably died in child-bed. The fact that he has a picture-book under his arm shows that there is another child to be thought of.'

I began to understand what my friend meant when he said that his brother possessed even keener faculties than he did himself. He glanced across at me and smiled. Mycroft took snuff from a tortoiseshell box and brushed away the wandering grains from his coat with a large red silk handkerchief.

'By the way, Sherlock,' said he, 'I have had something quite after your own heart – a most singular problem – submitted to my judgement. I really had not the energy to follow it up, save in a very incomplete fashion, but it gave me a basis for some very pleasing speculations. If you would care to hear the facts –'

'My dear Mycroft, I should be delighted.'

The brother scribbled a note upon a leaf of his pocket-book, and, ringing the bell, he handed it to the waiter.

'I have asked Mr Melas to step across,' said he. 'He lodges on the floor above me, and I have some slight acquaintance with him, which led him to come to me in his perplexity. Mr Melas is a Greek by extraction, as I understand, and he is a remarkable linguist. He earns his living partly as interpreter in the law courts, partly by acting as guide to any wealthy Orientals who may visit the Northumberland Avenue hotels. I think I will leave him to tell his own very remarkable experience in his own fashion.'

A few minutes later we were joined by a short, stout man, whose olive face and coal-black hair proclaimed his southern origin, though his speech was that of an educated Englishman. He shook hands eagerly with Sherlock Holmes, and his dark eyes sparkled with pleasure when he understood that the specialist was anxious to hear his story.

'I do not believe that the police credit me – on my word I do not,' said he, in a wailing voice. 'Just because they have never heard of it before, they think that such a thing cannot be. But I know that I shall never be easy in my mind until I know what has become of my poor man with the sticking-plaster upon his face.'

'I am all attention,' said Sherlock Holmes.

'This is Wednesday evening,' said Mr Melas; 'well, then, it was on Monday night – only two days ago, you understand – that all this happened. I am an interpreter, as, perhaps, my neighbour there has told you. I interpret all languages – or nearly all – but as I am a Greek by birth, and with a Grecian name, it is with that particular tongue that I am principally associated. For many years I have been the chief Greek interpreter in London, and my name is very well known in the hotels.

'It happens, not infrequently, that I am sent for at strange hours, by foreigners who get into difficulties, or by travellers who arrive late and wish my services. I was not surprised, therefore, on Monday night when a Mr Latimer, a very fashionably dressed young man, came up to my rooms and asked me to accompany him in a cab, which was waiting at the door. A Greek friend had come to see him upon business, he said, and, as he could speak nothing but his own tongue, the services of an interpreter were indispensable. He gave me to understand that his house was some little distance off, in Kensington, and he seemed to be in a great hurry, bustling me rapidly into the cab when we had descended into the street.

'I say into the cab, but I soon became doubtful as to whether it was not a carriage in which I had found myself. It was certainly more roomy than the ordinary four-wheeled disgrace to London, and the fittings, though frayed, were of rich quality. Mr Latimer seated himself opposite to me, and we started off through Charing Cross and up the Shaftesbury Avenue. We had come out upon

Oxford Street, and I had ventured some remark as to this being a roundabout way to Kensington, when my words were arrested by the extraordinary conduct of my companion.

'He began by drawing a most formidable-looking bludgeon loaded with lead from his pocket, and switched it backwards and forwards several times, as if to test its weight and strength. Then he placed it, without a word, upon the seat beside him. Having done this, he drew up the windows on each side, and I found to my astonishment that they were covered with paper so as to prevent my seeing through them.

'"I am sorry to cut off your view, Mr Melas," said he. "The fact is that I have no intention that you should see what the place is to which we are driving. It might possibly be inconvenient to me if you could find your way there again."

'As you can imagine, I was utterly taken aback by such an address. My companion was a powerful, broad-shouldered young fellow, and, apart from the weapon, I should not have had the slightest chance in a struggle with him.

'"This is very extraordinary conduct, Mr Latimer," I stammered. "You must be aware that what you are doing is quite illegal."

'"It is somewhat of a liberty, no doubt," said he, "but we'll make it up to you. But I must warn you, however, Mr Melas, that if at any time to-night you attempt to raise an alarm or do anything which is against my interests, you will find it a very serious thing. I beg you to remember that no one knows where you are, and that whether you are in this carriage or in my house, you are equally in my power."

'His words were quiet, but he had a rasping way of saying them which was very menacing. I sat in silence, wondering what on earth could be his reason for kidnapping me in this extraordinary fashion. Whatever it might be, it was perfectly clear that there was no possible use in my resisting, and that I could only wait to see what might befall.

'For nearly two hours we drove without my having the least clue as to where we were going. Sometimes the rattle of the stones told of a paved causeway, and at others our smooth, silent course suggested asphalt, but save this variation in sound there was nothing at all which could in the remotest way help me to form a guess as to where we were. The paper over each window was impenetrable to light, and a blue curtain was drawn across the glass-work in front. It was a quarter past seven when we left Pall Mall, and my watch showed me that it was ten minutes to nine when we at last came to a standstill. My companion let down the window and I caught a glimpse of a low, arched doorway with a lamp burning above it. As I was hurried from the carriage it swung open, and I found myself inside the house, with a vague impression of a lawn and trees on each side of me as I entered. Whether these were private grounds,

however, or *bona fide* country was more than I
could possibly venture to say.

'There was a coloured gas-lamp inside, which
was turned so low that I could see little save that
the hall was of some size and hung with pictures.
In the dim light I could make out that the person
who had opened the door was a small mean-
looking, middle-aged man with rounded shoulders.
As he turned towards us the glint of the light
showed me that he was wearing glasses.

'"Is this Mr Melas, Harold?" said he.

'"Yes."

'"Well done! Well done! No ill-will, Mr Melas,
I hope, but we could not get on without you. If
you deal fair with us you'll not regret it; but if you
try any tricks, God help you!"

'He spoke in a jerky, nervous fashion, and with
some giggling laughs in between, but somehow he
impressed me with fear more than the other.

'"What do you want with me?" I asked.

'"Only to ask a few questions of a Greek gentleman who is visiting us, and to let us have the
answers. But say no more than you are told to say,
or" – here came the nervous giggle again – "you
had better never have been born."

'As he spoke he opened a door and showed the
way into a room which appeared to be very richly
furnished – but again the only light was afforded
by a single lamp half turned down. The chamber
was certainly large, and the way in which my feet
sank into the carpet as I stepped across it told me

of its richness. I caught glimpses of velvet chairs, a high, white marble mantelpiece, and what seemed to be a suit of Japanese armour at one side of it. There was a chair just under the lamp, and the elderly man motioned that I should sit in it. The younger had left us, but he suddenly returned through another door, leading with him a gentleman clad in some sort of loose dressing-gown, who moved slowly towards us. As he came into the circle of dim light which enabled me to see him more clearly, I was thrilled with horror at his appearance. He was deadly pale and terribly emaciated, with the protruding, brilliant eyes of a man whose spirit is greater than his strength. But what shocked me more than any signs of physical weakness was that his face was grotesquely crisscrossed with sticking-plaster, and that one large pad of it was fastened over his mouth.

'"Have you the slate, Harold?" cried the older man, as this strange being fell rather than sat down into a chair. "Are his hands loose? Now then, give him the pencil. You are to ask the questions, Mr Melas, and he will write the answers. Ask him first of all whether he is prepared to sign the papers."

'The man's eyes flashed fire.

'"Never," he wrote in Greek upon the slate.

'"On no conditions?" I asked at the bidding of our tyrant.

'"Only if I see her married in my presence by a Greek priest whom I know."

'The man giggled in his venomous way.

'"You know what awaits you, then?"

'"I care nothing for myself."

'These are samples of the questions and answers which made up our strange, half-spoken, half-written conversation. Again and again I had to ask him whether he would give in and sign the document. Again and again I had the same indignant reply. But soon a happy thought came to me. I took to adding on little sentences of my own to each question – innocent ones at first, to test whether either of our companions knew anything of the matter, and then, as I found that they showed no sign, I played a more dangerous game. Our conversation ran something like this:

'"You can do no good by this obstinacy. *Who are you?*"

'"I care not. *I am a stranger in London*."

'"Your fate will be on your own head. *How long have you been here?*"

'"Let it be so. *Three weeks*."

'"This property can never be yours. *What ails you?*"

'"It shall not go to villains. *They are starving me*."

'"You shall go free if you sign. *What house is this?*"

'"I will never sign. *I do not know*."

'"You are not doing her any service. *What is your name?*"

'"Let me hear her say so. *Kratides*."

' "You shall see her if you sign. *Where are you from?*"

' "Then I shall never see her. *Athens.*"

'Another five minutes, Mr Holmes, and I should have wormed out the whole story under their very noses. My very next question might have cleared the matter up, but at that instant the door opened and a woman stepped into the room. I could not see her clearly enough to know more than that she was tall and graceful, with black hair, and clad in some sort of loose white gown.

' "Harold!" said she, speaking English with a broken accent. "I could not stay away longer. It is so lonely up there with only – oh, my God, it is Paul!"

'These last words were in Greek, and at the same instant the man, with a convulsive effort, tore the plaster from his lips, and screaming out "Sophy! Sophy!" rushed into the woman's arms. Their embrace was but for an instant, however, for the younger man seized the woman and pushed her out of the room, while the elder easily overpowered his emaciated victim, and dragged him away through the other door. For a moment I was left alone in the room, and I sprang to my feet with some vague idea that I might in some way get a clue to what this house was in which I found myself. Fortunately, however, I took no steps, for, looking up, I saw the older man was standing in the doorway, with his eyes fixed upon me.

' "That will do, Mr Melas," said he. "You

perceive that we have taken you into our confidence over some very private business. We should not have troubled you only that our friend who speaks Greek and who began these negotiations has been forced to return to the East. It was quite necessary for us to find someone to take his place, and we were fortunate in hearing of your powers."

'I bowed.

'"There are five sovereigns here," said he, walking up to me, "which will, I hope, be a sufficient fee. But remember," he added, tapping me lightly on the chest and giggling, "if you speak to a human soul about this – one human soul, mind – well, may God have mercy upon your soul!"

'I cannot tell you the loathing and horror with which this insignificant-looking man inspired me. I could see him better now as the lamp-light shone upon him. His features were peaky and sallow, and his little, pointed beard was thready and ill-nourished. He pushed his face forward as he spoke, and his lips and eyelids were continually twitching, like a man with St Vitus's Dance. I could not help thinking that this strange, catchy little laugh was also a symptom of some nervous malady. The terror of his face lay in his eyes, however, steel grey, and glistening coldly, with a malignant, inexorable cruelty in their depths.

'"We shall know if you speak of this," said he. "We have our own means of information. Now, you will find the carriage waiting, and my friend will see you on your way."

'I was hurried through the hall, and into the vehicle, again obtaining that momentary glimpse of trees and a garden. Mr Latimer followed closely at my heels, and took his place opposite to me without a word. In silence we again drove for an interminable distance, with the windows raised, until at last, just after midnight, the carriage pulled up.

'"You will get down here, Mr Melas," said my companion. "I am sorry to leave you so far from your house, but there is no alternative. Any attempt upon your part to follow the carriage can only end in injury to yourself."

'He opened the door as he spoke, and I had hardly time to spring out when the coachman lashed the horse, and the carriage rattled away. I looked round me in astonishment. I was on some sort of a heathy common, mottled over with dark clumps of furze bushes. Far away stretched a line of houses, with a light here and there in the upper windows. On the other side I saw the red signal lamps of a railway.

'The carriage which had brought me was already out of sight. I stood gazing round and wondering where on earth I might be, when I saw someone coming towards me in the darkness. As he came up to me I made out that it was a railway porter.

'"Can you tell me what place this is?" I asked.

'"Wandsworth Common," said he.

'"Can I get a train into town?"

'"If you walk on a mile or so, to Clapham Junction," said he, "you'll just be in time for the last to Victoria."

'So that was the end of my adventure, Mr Holmes. I do not know where I was nor whom I spoke with, nor anything, save what I have told you. But I know that there is foul play going on, and I want to help that unhappy man if I can. I told the whole story to Mr Mycroft Holmes next morning, and, subsequently, to the police.'

We all sat in silence for some little time after listening to this extraordinary narrative. Then Sherlock looked across at his brother.

'Any steps?' he asked.

Mycroft picked up the *Daily News*, which was lying on a side table.

'"Anybody supplying any information as to the whereabouts of a Greek gentleman named Paul Kratides, from Athens, who is unable to speak English, will be rewarded. A similar reward paid to anyone giving information about a Greek lady whose first name is Sophy. X 2473." That was in all the dailies. No answer.'

'How about the Greek Legation?'

'I have inquired. They know nothing.'

'A wire to the head of the Athens police, then.'

'Sherlock has all the energy of the family,' said Mycroft, turning to me. 'Well, you take up the case by all means, and let me know if you do any good.'

'Certainly,' answered my friend, rising from his

chair. 'I'll let you know, and Mr Melas also. In the meantime, Mr Melas, I should certainly be on my guard if I were you, for, of course, they must know through these advertisements that you have betrayed them.'

As we walked home together Holmes stopped at a telegraph office and sent off several wires.

'You see, Watson,' he remarked, 'our evening has been by no means wasted. Some of my most interesting cases have come to me in this way through Mycroft. The problem which we have just listened to, although it can admit of but one explanation, has still some distinguishing features.'

'You have hopes of solving it?'

'Well, knowing as much as we do, it will be singular indeed if we fail to discover the rest. You must yourself have formed some theory which will explain the facts to which we have listened.'

'In a vague way, yes.'

'What was your idea, then?'

'It seemed to me to be obvious that this Greek girl had been carried off by the young Englishman named Harold Latimer.'

'Carried off from where?'

'Athens, perhaps.'

Sherlock Holmes shook his head. 'This young man could not talk a word of Greek. The lady could talk English fairly well. Inference that she had been in England some little time, but he had not been in Greece.'

'Well, then, we will presume that she had come on a visit to England, and that this Harold had persuaded her to fly with him.'

'That is more probable.'

'Then the brother – for that, I fancy, must be the relationship – comes over from Greece to interfere. He imprudently puts himself into the power of the young man and his older associate. They seize him and use violence towards him in order to make him sign some papers to make over the girl's fortune – of which he may be trustee – to them. This he refuses to do. In order to negotiate with him, they have to get an interpreter, and they pitch upon this Mr Melas, having used some other one before. The girl is not told of the arrival of her brother, and finds it out by the merest accident.'

'Excellent, Watson,' cried Holmes. 'I really fancy that you are not far from the truth. You see that we hold all the cards, and we have only to fear some hidden act of violence on their part. If they give us time we must have them.'

'But how can we find where this house lies?'

'Well, if our conjecture is correct, and the girl's name is, or was, Sophy Kratides, we should have no difficulty in tracing her. That must be our main hope, for the brother, of course, is a complete stranger. It is clear that some time has elapsed since this Harold established these relations with the girl – some weeks at any rate – since the brother in Greece has had time to hear of it, and come across. If they have been living in the same place during this time, it is probable that we shall have some answer to Mycroft's advertisement.'

We had reached our house in Baker Street whilst we had been talking. Holmes ascended the stairs first, and as he opened the door of our room he gave a start of surprise. Looking over his shoulder I was equally astonished. His brother Mycroft was sitting smoking in the armchair.

'Come in, Sherlock! Come in, sir,' said he blandly, smiling at our surprised faces. 'You don't expect such energy from me, do you, Sherlock? But somehow this case attracts me.'

'How did you get here?'

'I passed you in a hansom.'

'There has been some new development?'

'I had an answer to my advertisement.'

'Ah!'

'Yes; it came within a few minutes of your leaving.'

'And to what effect?'

Mycroft Holmes took out a sheet of paper.

'Here it is,' said he, 'written with a J pen on royal cream paper, by a middle-aged man with a weak constitution. "Sir," he says, "in answer to your advertisement of today's date, I beg to inform you that I know the young lady in question very well. If you should care to call upon me, I could give you some particulars as to her painful history. She is living at present at The Myrtles, Beckenham. – Yours faithfully, J. DAVENPORT."

'He writes from Lower Brixton,' said Mycroft Holmes. 'Do you not think that we might drive to him now, Sherlock, and learn these particulars?'

'My dear Mycroft, the brother's life is more valuable than the sister's story. I think we should call at Scotland Yard for Inspector Gregson, and go straight out to Beckenham. We know that a man is being done to death, and every hour may be vital.'

'Better pick up Mr Melas upon our way,' I suggested; 'we may need an interpreter.'

'Excellent!' said Sherlock Holmes. 'Send the boy for a four-wheeler, and we shall be off at once.' He opened the table-drawer as he spoke, and I noticed that he slipped his revolver into his pocket. 'Yes,' said he, in answer to my glance, 'I should say from what we have heard that we are dealing with a particularly dangerous gang.'

It was almost dark before we found ourselves in Pall Mall, at the rooms of Mr Melas. A gentleman had just called for him, and he was gone.

'Can you tell me where?' asked Mycroft Holmes.

'I don't know, sir,' answered the woman who had opened the door. 'I only know that he drove away with the gentleman in a carriage.'

'Did the gentleman give a name?'

'No, sir.'

'He wasn't a tall, handsome, dark young man?'

'Oh, no, sir; he was a little gentleman, with

glasses, thin in the face, but very pleasant in his ways, for he was laughing all the time he was talking.'

'Come along!' cried Sherlock Holmes abruptly. 'This grows serious!' he observed, as we drove to Scotland Yard. 'These men have got hold of Melas again. He is a man of no physical courage, as they are well aware from their experience the other night. This villain was able to terrorize him the instant that he got into his presence. No doubt they want his professional services; but, having used him, they may be inclined to punish him for what they will regard as his treachery.'

Our hope was that by taking a train we might get to Beckenham as soon as, or sooner than, the carriage. On reaching Scotland Yard, however, it was more than an hour before we could get Inspector Gregson and comply with the legal formalities which would enable us to enter the house. It was a quarter to ten before we reached London Bridge, and half past before the four of us alighted on the Beckenham platform. A drive of half a mile brought us to The Myrtles – a large, dark house, standing back from the road in its own grounds. Here we dismissed our cab, and made our way up the drive together.

'The windows are all dark,' remarked the inspector. 'The house seems deserted.'

'Our birds are flown and the nest empty,' said Holmes.

'Why do you say so?'

'A carriage heavily loaded with luggage has passed out during the last hour.'

The inspector laughed. 'I saw the wheel-tracks in the light of the gate-lamp, but where does the luggage come in?'

'You may have observed the same wheel-tracks going the other way. But the outward-bound ones were very much deeper – so much so that we can say for a certainty that there was a very considerable weight on the carriage.'

'You get a trifle beyond me there,' said the inspector, shrugging his shoulders. 'It will not be an easy door to force. But we will try if we cannot make someone hear us.'

He hammered loudly at the knocker and pulled at the bell, but without any success. Holmes had slipped away, but he came back in a few minutes.

'I have a window open,' said he.

'It is a mercy that you are on the side of the force, and not against it, Mr Holmes,' remarked the inspector, as he noted the clever way in which my friend had forced back the catch. 'Well, I think that, under the circumstances, we may enter without waiting for an invitation.'

One after the other we made our way into a large apartment, which was evidently that in which Mr Melas had found himself. The inspector had lit his lantern, and by its light we could see the two doors, the curtain, the lamp and the suit of Japanese mail as he had described them. On the table stood two glasses, an empty brandy bottle, and the remains of a meal.

'What is that?' asked Holmes suddenly.

We all stood still and listened. A low, moaning sound was coming from somewhere above our heads. Holmes rushed to the door and out into the hall. The dismal noise came from upstairs. He dashed up, the inspector and I at his heels, while his brother, Mycroft, followed as quickly as his great bulk would permit.

Three doors faced us upon the second floor, and it was from the central of these that the sinister sounds were issuing, sinking sometimes into a dull mumble and rising again into a shrill whine. It was locked, but the key was on the outside. Holmes flung open the door and rushed in, but he was out again in an instant with his hand to his throat.

'It's charcoal!' he cried. 'Give it time. It will clear.'

Peering in, we could see that the only light in the room came from a dull, blue flame, which flickered from a small brass tripod in the centre. It threw a livid, unnatural circle upon the floor, while in the shadows beyond we saw the vague loom of two figures, which crouched against the wall. From the open door there reeked a horrible, poisonous exhalation, which set us gasping and coughing. Holmes rushed to the top of the stairs to draw in the fresh air, and then, dashing into the room, he threw up the window and hurled the brazen tripod out into the garden.

'We can enter in a minute,' he gasped, darting out again. 'Where is a candle? I doubt if we could strike a match in that atmosphere. Hold the light at the door and we shall get them out, Mycroft. Now!'

With a rush we got to the poisoned men and dragged them out on to the landing. Both of them were blue-lipped and insensible, with swollen, congested faces and protruding eyes. Indeed, so distorted were their features that, save for his black beard and stout figure, we might have failed to recognize in one of them the Greek interpreter who had parted from us only a few hours before at the Diogenes Club. His hands and feet were securely strapped together and he bore over one eye the mark of a violent blow. The other, who was secured in a similar fashion, was a tall man in the last stage of emaciation, with several strips of sticking-plaster arranged in a grotesque pattern over his face. He had ceased to moan as we laid him down, and a glance showed me that for him, at least, our aid had come too late. Mr Melas, however, still lived, and in less than an hour, with the aid of ammonia and brandy, I had the satisfaction of seeing him open his eyes, and of knowing that my hand had drawn him back from the dark valley in which all paths meet.

It was a simple story which he had to tell, and one which did but confirm our own deductions.

His visitor on entering his rooms had drawn a life preserver from his sleeve, and had so impressed him with the fear of instant and inevitable death, that he had kidnapped him for the second time. Indeed, it was almost mesmeric the effect which this giggling ruffian had produced upon the unfortunate linguist, for he could not speak of him save with trembling hands and a blanched cheek. He had been taken swiftly to Beckenham, and had acted as interpreter in a second interview, even more dramatic than the first, in which the two Englishmen had menaced their prisoner with instant death if he did not comply with their demands. Finally, finding him proof against every threat, they hurled him back into his prison, and after reproaching Melas with his treachery, which appeared from the newspaper advertisements, they had stunned him with a blow from a stick, and he remembered nothing more until he found us bending over him.

And this was the singular case of the Grecian Interpreter, the explanation of which is still involved in some mystery. We were able to find out, by communicating with the gentleman who had answered the advertisement, that the unfortunate young lady came of a wealthy Grecian family, and that she had been on a visit to some friends in England. While there she had met a young man named Harold Latimer, who had acquired an ascendancy over her and had eventually persuaded her to fly with him. Her friends, shocked at the event, had contented themselves with informing her brother at Athens, and had then washed their hands of the matter. The brother, on his arrival in England, had imprudently placed himself in the power of Latimer and of his associate, whose name was Wilson Kemp – a man of the foulest antecedents. These two, finding that through his ignorance of the language he was helpless in their hands, had kept him a prisoner, and had endeavoured, by cruelty and starvation, to make him sign away his own and his sister's property. They had kept him in the house without the girl's knowledge, and the plaster over the face had been for the purpose of making recognition difficult in case she should ever catch a glimpse of him. Her feminine perceptions, however, had instantly seen through the disguise when, on the occasion of the interpreter's first visit, she had seen him for the first time. The poor girl, however, was herself a prisoner, for there was no one about the house except the man who acted as coachman, and his wife, both of whom were tools of the conspirators. Finding that their secret was out and that their prisoner was not to be coerced, the two villains, with the girl, had fled away at a few hours' notice from the furnished house which they had hired, having first, as they thought, taken vengeance both upon the man who had defied and the one who had betrayed them.

Months afterwards a curious newspaper cutting reached us from Budapest. It told how two Englishmen who had been travelling with a woman had met with a tragic end. They had each been stabbed, it seems, and the Hungarian police were of opinion that they had quarrelled and had inflicted mortal injuries upon each other. Holmes, however, is, I fancy, of a different way of thinking, and he holds to this day that if one could find the Grecian girl one might learn how the wrongs of herself and her brother came to be avenged.

THE *GLORIA SCOTT*

'I have some papers here,' said my friend, Sherlock Holmes, as we sat one winter's night on either side of the fire, 'which I really think, Watson, it would be worth your while to glance over. These are the documents in the extraordinary case of the *Gloria Scott*, and this is the message which struck Justice of the Peace Trevor dead with horror when he read it.'

He had picked from a drawer a little tarnished cylinder, and, undoing the tape, he handed me a short note scrawled upon a half-sheet of slate-grey paper.

'The supply of game for London is going steadily up,' it ran. 'Head-keeper Hudson, we believe, has been now told to receive all orders for fly-paper, and for preservation of your hen pheasant's life.'

As I glanced up from reading this enigmatical message I saw Holmes chuckling at the expression upon my face.

'You look a little bewildered,' said he.

'I cannot see how such a message as this could inspire horror. It seems to me to be rather grotesque than otherwise.'

'Very likely. Yet the fact remains that the reader, who was a fine, robust old man, was knocked clean down by it, as if it had been the butt-end of a pistol.'

'You arouse my curiosity,' said I. 'But why did you say just now that there were very particular reasons why I should study this case?'

'Because it was the first in which I was ever engaged.'

I had often endeavoured to elicit from my companion what had first turned his mind in the direction of criminal research, but I had never caught him before in a communicative humour. Now he sat forward in his armchair, and spread out the documents upon his knees. Then he lit his pipe and sat for some time smoking and turning them over.

'You never heard me talk of Victor Trevor?' he asked. 'He was the only friend I made during the two years that I was at college. I was never a very sociable fellow, Watson, always rather fond of moping in my rooms and working out my own little methods of thought, so that I never mixed much with the men of my year. Bar fencing and boxing I had few athletic tastes, and then my line of study was quite distinct from that of the other fellows, so that we had no points of contact at all. Trevor was the only man I knew, and that only through the accident of his bull-terrier freezing on to my ankle one morning as I went down to chapel.

'It was a prosaic way of forming a friendship, but it was effective. I was laid by the heels for ten days, and Trevor used to come in to inquire after me. At first it was only a minute's chat, but soon his visits lengthened, and before the end of the term we were close friends. He was a hearty, full-blooded fellow, full of spirit and energy, the very opposite to me in most respects; but we found we had some subjects in common, and it was a bond of union when I learned that he was as friendless as I. Finally, he invited me down to his father's place at Donnithorpe, in Norfolk, and I accepted his hospitality for a month of the long vacation.

'Old Trevor was evidently a man of some wealth and consideration, a J.P. and a landed proprietor. Donnithorpe is a little hamlet just to the north of Langmere, in the country of the Broads. The house was an old-fashioned, widespread, oak-beamed, brick building, with a fine lime-lined avenue leading up to it. There was excellent wild-duck shooting in the fens, remarkably good fishing, a small but select library, taken over, as I understood, from a former occupant, and a tolerable cook, so that it would be a fastidious man who could not put in a pleasant month there.

'Trevor senior was a widower, and my friend was his only son. There had been a daughter, I heard, but she had died of diphtheria while on a visit to Birmingham. The father interested me extremely. He was a man of little culture, but with a considerable amount of rude strength both physically and mentally. He knew hardly any books, but he had travelled far, had seen much of the world, and had remembered all that he had learned. In person he was a thick-set, burly man with a shock of grizzled hair, a brown, weather-beaten face, and blue eyes which were keen to the verge of fierceness. Yet he had a reputation for kindness and charity in the countryside, and was noted for the leniency of his sentences from the bench.

'One evening, shortly after my arrival, we were sitting over a glass of port after dinner, when young Trevor began to talk about those habits of observation and inference which I had already formed into a system, although I had not yet appreciated the part which they were to play in my life. The old man evidently thought that his son was exaggerating in his description of one or two trivial feats which I had performed.

'"Come now, Mr Holmes," said he, laughing good-humouredly, "I'm an excellent subject, if you can deduce anything from me."

'"I fear there is not very much," I answered. "I might suggest that you have gone about in fear of some personal attack within the last twelve months."

'The laugh faded from his lips, and he stared at me in great surprise.

'"Well, that's true enough," said he. "You know Victor," turning to his son, "when we broke up that poaching gang, they swore to knife us; and Sir Edward Hoby has actually been attacked. I've always been on my guard since then, though I have no idea how you know it."

'"You have a very handsome stick," I answered. "By the inscription, I observed that you had not had it more than a year. But you have taken some pains to bore the head of it and pour melted lead into the hole, so as to make it a formidable weapon. I argued that you would not take such precautions unless you had some danger to fear."

'"Anything else?' he asked, smiling.

'"You have boxed a good deal in your youth."

'"Right again. How did you know it? Is my nose knocked a little out of the straight?"

'"No," said I, "it is your ears. They have the peculiar flattening and thickening which marks the boxing man."

'"Anything else?"

'"You have done a great deal of digging, by your callosities."

'"Made all my money at the gold-fields."

'"You have been in New Zealand."

'"Right again."

'"You have visited Japan."

'"Quite true."

'"And you have been most intimately associated with someone whose initials were J.A., and whom you afterwards were eager to entirely forget."

'Mr Trevor stood slowly up, fixed his large blue eyes on me with a strange, wild stare, and then pitched forward on his face among the nut-shells which strewed the cloth, in a dead faint.

'You can imagine, Watson, how shocked both his son and I were. His attack did not last long, however, for when we undid his collar and sprinkled the water from one of the finger glasses over his face, he gave a gasp or two and sat up.

'"Ah, boys!" said he, forcing a smile. "I hope I haven't frightened you. Strong as I look, there is a weak place in my heart, and it does not take much to knock me over. I don't know how you manage this, Mr Holmes, but it seems to me that all the detectives of fact and of fancy would be children in your hands. That's your line of life, sir, and you may take the word of a man who has seen something of the world."

'And that recommendation, with the exaggerated estimate of my ability with which he prefaced it, was, if you will believe me, Watson, the very first thing which ever made me feel that a profession might be made out of what had up to that time been the merest hobby. At the moment, however, I was too much concerned at the sudden illness of my host to think of anything else.

'"I hope that I have said nothing to pain you," said I.

'"Well, you certainly touched upon rather a tender point. Might I ask how you know and how much you know?" He spoke now in a half-jesting fashion, but a look of terror still lurked at the back of his eyes.

'"It is simplicity itself," said I. "When you bared your arm to draw that fish into the boat, I saw that 'J.A.' had been tattooed in the bend of the elbow. The letters were still legible, but it was perfectly clear from their blurred appearance, and from the staining of the skin round them, that efforts had been made to obliterate them. It was obvious, then, that those initials had once been very familiar to you, and that you had afterwards wished to forget them."

'"What an eye you have!" he cried, with a sigh of relief. "It is just as you say. But we won't talk of it. Of all ghosts the ghosts of our old loves are the worst. Come into the billiard-room and have a quiet cigar."

'From that day, amid all his cordiality, there was always a touch of suspicion in Mr Trevor's manner towards me. Even his son remarked it. "You've given the governor such a turn," said he, "that he'll never be sure again of what you know and what you don't know." He did not mean to show it, I am sure, but it was so strongly in his mind that it peeped out at every action. At last I became so convinced that I was causing him uneasiness, that I drew my visit to a close. On the very day, however, before I left, an incident occurred which proved in the sequel to be of importance.

'We were sitting upon the lawn on garden chairs, the three of us, basking in the sun and admiring the view across the Broads, when the maid came out to say that there was a man at the door who wanted to see Mr Trevor.

'"What is his name?" asked my host.

'"He would not give any."

'"What does he want, then?"

'"He says that you know him, and that he only wants a moment's conversation."

'"Show him round here." An instant afterwards there appeared a little weazened fellow, with a cringing manner and a shambling style of walking. He wore an open jacket, with a splotch of tar on the sleeve, a red and black check shirt, dungaree trousers, and heavy boots badly worn. His face was thin and brown and crafty, with a perpetual smile upon it, which showed an irregular line of yellow teeth, and his crinkled hands were half closed in a way that is distinctive of sailors. As he came slouching across the lawn I heard Mr Trevor make a sort of hiccuping noise in his throat, and, jumping out of his chair, he ran into the house. He was back in a moment, and I smelt a strong reek of brandy as he passed me.

'"Well, my man," said he, "what can I do for you?"

'The sailor stood looking at him with puckered eyes, and with the same loose-lipped smile upon his face.

'"You don't know me?" he asked.

'"Why, dear me, it is surely Hudson!" said Mr Trevor, in a tone of surprise.

'"Hudson it is, sir," said the seaman. "Why,

it's thirty year and more since I saw you last. Here you are in your house, and me still picking my salt meat out of the harness cask."

'"Tut, you will find that I have not forgotten old times," cried Mr Trevor, and, walking towards the sailor, he said something in a low voice. "Go into the kitchen," he continued out loud, "and you will get food and drink. I have no doubt that I shall find you a situation."

'"Thank you, sir," said the seaman, touching his forelock. "I'm just off a two-yearer in an eight-knot tramp, short-handed at that, and I wants a rest. I thought I'd get it either with Mr Beddoes or with you."

'"Ah!" cried Mr Trevor, "you know where Mr Beddoes is?"

'"Bless you, sir, I know where all my old friends are," said the fellow, with a sinister smile, and slouched off after the maid to the kitchen. Mr Trevor mumbled something to us about having been shipmates with the man when he was going back to the diggings, and then, leaving us on the lawn, he went indoors. An hour later, when we entered the house we found him stretched dead drunk upon the dining-room sofa. The whole incident left a most ugly impression upon my mind, and I was not sorry next day to leave Donnithorpe behind me, for I felt that my presence must be a source of embarrassment to my friend.

'All this occurred during the first month of the long vacation. I went up to my London rooms, where I spent seven weeks working out a few experiments in organic chemistry. One day, however, when the autumn was far advanced and the vacation drawing to a close, I received a telegram from my friend imploring me to return to Donnithorpe, and saying that he was in great need of my advice and assistance. Of course I dropped everything and set out for the north once more.

'He met me with the dog-cart at the station, and I saw at a glance that the last two months had been very trying ones for him. He had grown thin and careworn, and had lost the loud, cheery manner for which he had been remarkable.

'"The governor is dying," were the first words he said.

'"Impossible!" I cried. "What is the matter?"

'"Apoplexy. Nervous shock. He's been on the verge all day. I doubt if we shall find him alive."

'I was, as you may think, Watson, horrified at this unexpected news.

'"What has caused it?" I said.

'"Ah, that is the point. Jump in, and we can talk it over while we drive. You remember that fellow who came upon the evening before you left us?"

'"Perfectly."

'"Do you know who it was that we let into the house that day?"

'"I have no idea."

'"It was the Devil, Holmes!" he cried.

'I stared at him in astonishment.

'"Yes; it was the Devil himself. We have not had a peaceful hour since – not one. The governor has never held up his head from that evening, and now the life has been crushed out of him, and his heart broken, all through this accursed Hudson.'

'"What power had he, then?"

'"Ah, that is what I would give so much to know. The kindly, charitable, good old governor! How could he have fallen into the clutches of such a ruffian? But I am so glad that you have come, Holmes. I trust very much to your judgement and discretion, and I know that you will advise me for the best."

'We were dashing along the smooth, white country road, with a long stretch of Broads in front of us glimmering in the red light of the setting sun. From a grove upon our left I could already see the high chimneys and the flagstaff which marked the squire's dwelling.

'"My father made the fellow gardener," said my companion, "and then, as that did not satisfy him, he was promoted to be butler. The house seemed to be at his mercy, and he wandered about and did what he chose in it. The maids complained of his drunken habits and his vile language. The dad raised their wages all round to recompense them for the annoyance. The fellow would take the boat and my father's best gun and treat himself to little shooting parties. And all this with such a sneering, leering, insolent face, that I would have knocked him down twenty times over if he had been a man of my own age. I tell you, Holmes, I have had to keep a tight hold upon myself all this time, and now I am asking myself whether, if I had let myself go a little more, I might not have been a wiser man.

'"Well, matters went from bad to worse with us, and this animal, Hudson, became more and more intrusive, until at last, on his making some insolent reply to my father in my presence one day, I took him by the shoulder and turned him out of the room. He slunk away with a livid face, and two venomous eyes which uttered more threats than his tongue could do. I don't know what passed between the poor dad and him after that, but the dad came to me next day and asked me whether I would mind apologizing to Hudson. I refused, as you can imagine, and asked my father how he could allow such a wretch to take such liberties with himself and his household.

'"Ah, my boy," said he, "it is all very well to talk, but you don't know how I am placed. But you shall know, Victor. I'll see that you shall know, come what may! You wouldn't believe harm of your poor old father, would you, lad?" He was very much moved, and shut himself up in the study all day, where I could see through the window that he was writing busily.

'"That evening there came what seemed to be a grand release, for Hudson told us that he was going to leave us. He walked into the dining-room as we sat after dinner and announced his intention in the thick voice of a half-drunken man.

'"I've had enough of Norfolk," said he. "I'll run down to Mr Beddoes, in Hampshire. He'll be as glad to see me as you were, I dare say."

'"You're not going away in an unkind spirit, Hudson, I hope?" said my father, with a tameness which made my blood boil.

'"I've not had my 'pology," said he sulkily, glancing in my direction.

'"Victor, you will acknowledge that you have used this worthy fellow rather roughly?" said the dad, turning to me.

'"On the contrary, I think that we have both shown extraordinary patience towards him," I answered.

'"Oh, you do, do you?" he snarled. "Very good, mate. We'll see about that!" He slouched out of the room, and half an hour afterwards left the house, leaving my father in a state of pitiable nervousness. Night after night I heard him pacing his room, and it was just as he was recovering his confidence that the blow did at last fall.

'"And how?" I asked eagerly.

'"In a most extraordinary fashion. A letter arrived for my father yesterday evening, bearing the Fordingbridge postmark. My father read it, clapped both his hands to his head, and began running round the room in little circles like a man who has been driven out of his senses. When I at last drew him down on to the sofa, his mouth and eyelids were all puckered on one side, and I saw that he had had a stroke. Dr Fordham came over at once, and we put him to bed; but the paralysis has spread, he has shown no sign of returning consciousness, and I think that we shall hardly find him alive."

'"You horrify me, Trevor!" I cried. "What, then, could have been in this letter to cause so dreadful a result?"

'"Nothing. There lies the inexplicable part of it. The message was absurd and trivial. Ah, my God, it is as I feared!"

'As he spoke we came round the curve of the avenue, and saw in the fading light that every blind in the house had been drawn down. As we dashed up to the door, my friend's face convulsed with grief, a gentleman in black emerged from it.

'"When did it happen, doctor?" asked Trevor.

'"Almost immediately after you left."

'"Did he recover consciousness?"

'"For an instant before the end."

'"Any message for me?"

'"Only that the papers were in the back drawer of the Japanese cabinet."

'My friend ascended with the doctor to the chamber of death, while I remained in the study, turning the whole matter over and over in my head, and feeling as sombre as ever I had done in my life. What was the past of this Trevor: pugilist, traveller, and gold-digger; and how had he placed himself in the power of this acid-faced seaman?

Why, too, should he faint at an allusion to the half-effaced initials upon his arm, and die of fright when he had a letter from Fordingbridge? Then I remembered that Fordingbridge was in Hampshire, and that this Mr Beddoes, whom the seaman had gone to visit, and presumably to blackmail, had also been mentioned as living in Hampshire. The letter, then, might either come from Hudson, the seaman, saying that he had betrayed the guilty secret which appeared to exist, or it might come from Beddoes, warning an old confederate that such a betrayal was imminent. So far it seemed clear enough. But, then, how could the letter be trivial and grotesque as described by the son? He must have misread it. If so, it must have been one of those ingenious secret codes which mean one thing while they seem to mean another. I must see this letter. If there were a hidden meaning in it, I was confident that I could pluck it forth. For an hour I sat pondering over it in the gloom, until at last a weeping maid brought in a lamp, and close at her heels came my friend Trevor, pale and composed, with these very papers, which lie upon my knee, held in his grasp. He sat down opposite to me, drew the lamp to the edge of the table, and handed me a short note scribbled, as you see, upon a single sheet of grey paper. "The supply of game for London is going steadily up," it ran. "Head-keeper Hudson, we believe, has been now told to receive all orders for fly-paper and for preservation of your hen pheasant's life."

'I dare say my face looked as bewildered as yours did just now when first I read this message. Then I re-read it very carefully. It was evidently as I had thought, and some second meaning must be buried in this strange combination of words. Or could it be that there was a prearranged signifi-cance to such phrases as "fly-paper" and "hen-pheasant"? Such a meaning would be arbitrary, and could not be deduced in any way. And yet I was loath to believe that this was the case, and the presence of the word "Hudson" seemed to show that the subject of the message was as I had guessed, and that it was from Beddoes rather than the sailor. I tried it backwards, but the combina-tion, "Life pheasant's hen", was not encouraging. Then I tried alternate words, but neither "The of for" nor "supply game London" promised to throw any light upon it. Then in an instant the key of the riddle was in my hands, and I saw that every third word beginning with the first would give a message which might well drive old Trevor to despair.

'It was short and terse, the warning, as I now read it to my companion:

'"The game is up. Hudson has told all. Fly for your life."

'Victor Trevor sank his face into his shaking hands. "It must be that, I suppose," said he. "This is worse than death, for it means disgrace as well. But what is the meaning of these 'head-keepers' and 'hen pheasants'?"

'"It means nothing to the message, but it might mean a good deal to us if we had no other means of discovering the sender. You see that he has begun by writing, 'The ... game ... is,' and so on. Afterwards he had, to fulfil the prearranged cipher, to fill in any two words in each space. He would naturally use the first words which came to his mind, and if there were so many which referred to sport among them, you may be tolerably sure that he is either an ardent shot or interested in breeding. Do you know anything of this Beddoes?"

'"Why, now that you mention it," said he, "I remember that my poor father used to have an invitation from him to shoot over his preserves every autumn."

'"Then it is undoubtedly from him that the note comes," said I. "It only remains for us to find out what this secret was which the sailor Hudson seems to have held over the heads of these two wealthy and respected men."

'"Alas, Holmes, I fear that it is one of sin and shame!" cried my friend. "But from you I shall have no secrets. Here is the statement which was drawn up by my father when he knew that the danger from Hudson had become imminent. I found it in the Japanese cabinet, as he told the doctor. Take it and read it to me, for I have neither the strength nor the courage to do it myself."

'These are the very papers, Watson, which he

handed to me, and I will read them to you as I read them in the old study that night to him. They are endorsed outside as you see: "Some particulars of the voyage of the barque *Gloria Scott*, from her leaving Falmouth on the 8th October, 1855, to her destruction in N. lat. 15° 29', W. long. 25° 14', on November 6th." It is in the form of a letter, and runs in this way:

'My dear, dear son, – Now that approaching disgrace begins to darken the closing years of my life, I can write with all truth and honesty that it is not the terror of the law, it is not the loss of my position in the county, nor is it my fall in the eyes of all who have known me, which cuts me to the heart; but it is the thought that you should come to blush for me – you who love me, and who have seldom, I hope, had reason to do other than respect me. But if the blow falls which is for ever hanging over me, then I should wish you to read this that you may know straight from me how far I have been to blame. On the other hand, if all should go well (which may kind God Almighty grant!), then if by any chance this paper should be still undestroyed, and should fall into your hands, I conjure you by all you hold sacred, by the memory of your dear mother, and by the love which has been between us, to hurl it into the fire, and to never give one thought to it again.

'If, then, your eye goes on to read this line, I know that I shall already have been exposed and dragged from my home, or, as is more likely – for you know that my heart is weak – be lying with my tongue sealed for ever in death. In either case the time for suppression is past, and every word which I tell you is the naked truth; and this I swear as I hope for mercy.

'My name, dear lad, is not Trevor. I was James Armitage in my younger days, and you can understand now the shock that it was to me a few weeks ago when your college friend addressed me in words which seemed to imply that he had surmised my secret. As Armitage it was that I entered a London banking house, and as Armitage I was convicted of breaking my country's laws, and was sentenced to transportation. Do not think very harshly of me, laddie. It was a debt of honour, so-called, which I had to pay, and I used money which was not my own to do it, in the certainty that I could replace it before there could be any possibility of its being missed. But the most dreadful ill-luck pursued me. The money which I had reckoned upon never came to hand, and a premature examination of accounts exposed my deficit. The case might have been dealt leniently with, but the laws were more harshly administered thirty years ago than now, and on my twenty-third birthday I found myself chained as a felon with thirty-seven other convicts in the 'tween decks of the barque *Gloria Scott*, bound for Australia.

'It was the year '55, when the Crimean War was at its height, and the old convict ships had been largely used as transports in the Black Sea. The Government was compelled therefore to use smaller and less suitable vessels for sending out their prisoners. The *Gloria Scott* had been in the Chinese tea trade, but she was an old-fashioned, heavy-bowed, broad-beamed craft, and the new clippers had cut her out. She was a 500-ton boat, and besides her thirty-eight jail birds, she carried twenty-six of a crew, eighteen soldiers, a captain, three mates, a doctor, a chaplain, and four warders. Nearly a hundred souls were in her, all told, when we set sail from Falmouth.

'The partitions between the cells of the convicts, instead of being of thick oak, as is usual to convict ships, were quite thin and frail. The man next to me upon the aft side was one whom I had particularly noticed when we were led down to the quay. He was a young man with a clear, hairless face, a long thin nose, and rather nutcracker jaws. He carried his head very jauntily in the air, had a swaggering style of walking, and was above all else remarkable for his extraordinary height. I don't think any of our heads would come up to his shoulder, and I am sure that he could not have measured less than six and a half feet. It was strange among so many sad and weary faces to see one which was full of energy and resolution. The sight of it was to me like a fire in a snowstorm. I was glad then to find that he was my neighbour, and gladder still when, in the dead of the night, I heard a whisper close to my ear, and found that he had managed to cut an opening in the board which separated us.

'"Halloa, chummy!" said he, "what's your name, and what are you here for?"

'I answered him, and asked in turn who I was talking with.

'"I'm Jack Prendergast," said he, "and, by God, you'll learn to bless my name before you've done with me!"

'I remembered hearing of his case, for it was one which had made an immense sensation throughout the country, some time before my own arrest. He was a man of good family and of great ability, but of incurably vicious habits, who had, by an ingenious system of fraud, obtained huge sums of money from the leading London merchants.

'"Ah, ah! You remember my case?" said he, proudly.

'"Very well indeed."

'"Then maybe you remember something queer about it?"

'"What was that, then?"

'"I had nearly a quarter of a million, hadn't I?"

'"So it was said."

'"But none was recovered, eh?"

'"No."

'"Well, where d'ye suppose the balance is?" he asked.

'"I have no idea," said I.

'"Right between my finger and thumb," he

cried. "By God, I've got more pounds to my name than you have hairs on your head. And if you've money, my son, and know how to handle it and spread it, you can do *anything*! Now, you don't think it likely that a man who could do anything is going to wear his breeches out sitting in the stinking hold of a rat-gutted, beetle-ridden, mouldy old coffin of a China coaster? No, sir, such a man will look after himself, and will look after his chums. You may lay to that! You hold on to him, and you may kiss the Book that he'll haul you through."

'That was his style of talk, and at first I thought it meant nothing, but after a while, when he had tested me and sworn me in with all possible solemnity, he let me understand that there really was a plot to gain command of the vessel. A dozen of the prisoners had hatched it before they came aboard: Prendergast was the leader, and his money was the motive power.

'"I'd a partner," said he, "a rare good man, as true as a stock to a barrel. He's got the dibs, he has, and where do you think he is at this moment? Why, he's the chaplain of this ship – the chaplain, no less! He came aboard with a black coat and his papers right, and money enough in his box to buy the thing right from keep to maintruck. The crew are his, body and soul. He could buy 'em at so much a gross with a cash discount, and he did it before ever they signed on. He's got two of the warders and Mercer the second mate, and he'd get the captain himself if he thought him worth it."

'"What are we to do, then?" I asked.

'"What do you think?" said he. "We'll make the coats of some of these soldiers redder than ever the tailor did."

'"But they are armed," said I.

'"And so shall we be, my boy. There's a brace of pistols for every mother's son of us, and if we can't carry this ship, with the crew at our back, it's time we were all sent to a young Miss's boarding school. You speak to your mate on the left tonight, and see if he is to be trusted."

'I did so, and found my other neighbour to be a young fellow in much the same position as myself, whose crime had been forgery. His name was Evans but he afterwards changed it, like myself, and he is now a rich and prosperous man in the South of England. He was ready enough to join the conspiracy, as the only means of saving ourselves, and before we had crossed the Bay there were only two of the prisoners who were not in the secret. One of these was of weak mind, and we did not dare to trust him, and the other was suffering from jaundice, and could not be of any use to us.

'From the beginning there was really nothing to prevent us taking possession of the ship. The crew were a set of ruffians, specially picked for the job. The sham chaplain came into our cells to exhort us, carrying a black bag, supposed to be full of tracts; and so often did he come that by the third day wc had each stowed away at the foot of our bed a file, a brace of pistols, a pound of powder, and twenty slugs. Two of the warders were agents of Prendergast, and the second mate was his right-hand man. The captain, the two mates, two warders, Lieutenant Martin, his eighteen soldiers, and the doctor were all that we had against us. Yet, safe as it was, we determined to neglect no precaution, and to make our attack suddenly at night. It came, however, more quickly than we expected, and in this way:

'One evening, about the third week after our start, the doctor had come down to see one of the prisoners, who was ill, and, putting his hand down the bottom of his bunk, he felt the outline of the pistols. If he had been silent he might have blown the whole thing; but he was a nervous little chap, so he gave a cry of surprise and turned so pale, that the man knew what was up in an instant and seized him. He was gagged before he could give the alarm, and tied down upon the bed. He had unlocked the door that led to the deck, and we were through it in a rush. The two sentries were shot down, and so was a corporal who came running to see what was the matter. There were two more soldiers at the door of the state-room, and their muskets seemed not to be loaded, for they never fired upon us, and they were shot while trying to fix their bayonets. Then we rushed on into the captain's cabin, but as we pushed open

the door there was an explosion from within, and
there he lay with his head on the chart of the
Atlantic, which was pinned upon the table, while
the chaplain stood, with a smoking pistol in his
hand, at his elbow. The two mates had both been
seized by the crew, and the whole business seemed
to be settled.

'The state-room was next the cabin, and we
flocked in there and flopped down on the settees,
all speaking together, for we were just mad with
the feeling that we were free once more. There
were lockers all round, and Wilson, the sham
chaplain, knocked one of them in, and pulled out
a dozen of brown sherry. We cracked off the
necks of the bottles, poured the stuff out into
tumblers, and were just tossing them off, when in
an instant, without warning, there came a roar of
muskets in our ears, and the saloon was so full of
smoke that we could not see across the table.
When it cleared away again the place was a
shambles. Wilson and eight others were wriggling
on the top of each other on the floor, and the blood
and brown sherry on that table turn me sick now
when I think of it. We were so cowed by the sight
that I think we should have given the job up if it
had not been for Prendergast. He bellowed like
a bull and rushed for the door with all that were
left alive at his heels. Out we ran, and there on
the poop were the lieutenant and ten of his men.
The swing skylights above the saloon table had
been a bit open, and they had fired on us through

the slit. We got on them before they could load, and they stood to it like men, but we had the upper hand of them, and in five minutes it was all over. My God! was there ever a slaughter-house like that ship? Prendergast was like a raging devil, and he picked the soldiers up as if they had been children and threw them overboard, alive or dead. There was one sergeant that was horribly wounded, and yet kept on swimming for a surprising time, until someone in mercy blew out his brains. When the fighting was over there was no one left of our enemies except just the warders, the mates, and the doctor.

'It was over them that the great quarrel arose. There were many of us who were glad enough to win back our freedom, and yet who had no wish to have murder on our souls. It was one thing to knock the soldiers over with their muskets in their hands, and it was another to stand by while men were being killed in cold blood. Eight of us, five convicts and three sailors, said that we would not see it done. But there was no moving Prendergast and those who were with him. Our only chance of safety lay in making a clean job of it, said he, and he would not leave a tongue with power to wag in a witness-box. It nearly came to our sharing the fate of the prisoners, but at last he said that if we wished we might take a boat and go. We jumped at the offer, for we were already sick of these bloodthirsty doings, and we saw that there would be worse before it was done. We were given a suit of sailor's togs each, a barrel of water, two casks, one of junk and one of biscuits, and a compass. Prendergast threw us over a chart, told us that we were shipwrecked mariners whose ship had foundered in lat. 15°N. and long. 25°W., and then cut the painter and let us go.

'And now I come to the most surprising part of my story, my dear son. The seamen had hauled the foreyard aback during the rising, but now as we left them they brought it square again, and, as there was a light wind from the north and east, the barque began to draw slowly away from us. Our boat lay, rising and falling, upon the long, smooth rollers, and Evans and I, who were the most educated of the party, were sitting in the sheets working out our position and planning what coast we should make for. It was a nice question, for the Cape of Verde was about 500 miles to the north of us, and the African coast about 700 miles to the east. On the whole, as the wind was coming round to north, we thought that Sierra Leone might be best, and turned our head in that direction, the barque being at that time nearly hull down on our starboard quarter. Suddenly as we looked at her we saw a dense black cloud of smoke shoot up from her, which hung like a monstrous tree upon the skyline. A few seconds later a roar like thunder burst upon our ears, and as the smoke thinned away there was no sign left of the *Gloria Scott*. In an instant we swept the boat's head round again, and pulled with all our strength for the place where the haze, still trailing over the water, marked the scene of this catastrophe.

'It was a long hour before we reached it, and at first we feared we had come too late to save anyone. A splintered boat and a number of crates and fragments of spars rising and falling on the waves showed us where the vessel had foundered, but there was no sign of life, and we had turned away in despair when we heard a cry for help, and saw at some distance a piece of wreckage with a man lying stretched across it. When we pulled him aboard the boat he proved to be a young seaman of the name of Hudson, who was so burned and exhausted that he could give us no account of what had happened until the following morning.

'It seemed that after we had left, Prendergast and his gang had proceeded to put to death the five remaining prisoners: the two warders had been shot and thrown overboard, and so also had the third mate. Prendergast then descended into the 'tween decks, and with his own hands cut the throat of the unfortunate surgeon. There only remained the first mate, who was a bold and active man. When he saw the convict approaching him with the bloody knife in his hand, he kicked off his bonds, which he had somehow contrived to loosen, and rushing down the deck he plunged into the afterhold.

'A dozen convicts who descended with their pistols in search of him found him with a matchbox in his hand seated beside an open powder barrel, which was one of a hundred carried on board, and swearing that he would blow all hands up if he were in any way molested. An instant later the explosion occurred, though Hudson thought it was caused by the misdirected bullet of one of the convicts rather than the mate's match. Be the cause what it may, it was the end of the *Gloria Scott*, and of the rabble who held command of her.

'Such, in a few words, my dear boy, is the history of this terrible business in which I was involved. Next day we were picked up by the brig *Hotspur*, bound for Australia, whose captain found no difficulty in believing that we were the survivors of a passenger ship which had foundered. The transport ship, *Gloria Scott*, was set down by the Admiralty as being lost at sea, and no word has ever leaked out as to her true fate. After an excellent voyage the *Hotspur* landed us at Sydney, where Evans and I changed our names and made our way to the diggings, where among the crowds who were gathered from all nations, we had no difficulty in losing our former identities.

'The rest I need not relate. We prospered, we travelled, we came back as rich colonials to England, and we bought country estates. For more than twenty years we have led peaceful and useful lives, and we hoped that our past was for ever buried. Imagine, then, my feelings when in the seaman who came to us I recognized instantly the man who had been picked off the wreck! He had tracked us down somehow, and had set himself to live upon our fears. You will understand now how it was that I strove to keep peace with him, and you will in some measure sympathize with me in the fears which fill me, now that he has gone from me to his other victim with threats upon his tongue.'

'Underneath is written, in a hand so shaky as to be hardly legible, "Beddoes writes in cipher to say that H. has told all. Sweet Lord, have mercy on our souls!"

'That was the narrative which I read that night to young Trevor, and I think, Watson, that under the circumstances it was a dramatic one. The good fellow was heartbroken at it, and went out to the Terai tea planting, where I hear that he is doing well. As to the sailor and Beddoes, neither of them was ever heard of again after that day on which the letter of warning was written. They both disappeared utterly and completely. No complaint had been lodged with the police, so that Beddoes had mistaken a threat for a deed. Hudson had been seen lurking about, and it was believed by the police that he had done away with Beddoes, and had fled. For myself, I believe that the truth was exactly the opposite. I think it is most probable that Beddoes, pushed to desperation, and believing himself to have been already betrayed, had revenged himself upon Hudson, and had fled from the country with as much money as he could lay his hands on. Those are the facts of the case, Doctor, and if they are of any use to your collection, I am sure that they are very heartily at your service.'

THE RESIDENT PATIENT

In glancing over the somewhat incoherent series of memoirs with which I have endeavoured to illustrate a few of the mental peculiarities of my friend, Mr Sherlock Holmes, I have been struck by the difficulty which I have experienced in picking out examples which shall in every way answer my purpose. For in those cases in which Holmes has performed some *tour de force* of analytical reasoning, and has demonstrated the value of his peculiar methods of investigation, the facts themselves have often been so slight or so commonplace that I could not feel justified in laying them before the public. On the other hand, it has frequently happened that he has been concerned in some research where the facts have been of the most remarkable and dramatic character, but where the share which he has himself taken in determining their causes has been less pronounced than I, as his biographer, could wish. The small matter which I have chronicled under the heading of *A Study in Scarlet*, and that other later one connected with the loss of the *Gloria Scott*, may serve as examples of this Scylla and Charybdis which are for ever threatening his historian. It may be that, in the business of which I am now about to write, the part which my friend played is not sufficiently accentuated; and yet the whole train of circumstances is so remarkable that I cannot bring myself to omit it entirely from this series.

It had been a close, rainy day in August. Our blinds were half drawn, and Holmes lay curled upon the sofa, reading and re-reading a letter which he had received by the morning post. For myself, my term of service in India had trained me to stand heat better than cold, and a thermometer of 90 was no hardship. But the paper was uninteresting. Parliament had risen. Everybody was out of town, and I yearned for the glades of the New Forest or the shingle of Southsea. A depleted bank account had caused me to postpone my holiday, and as to my companion, neither the country nor the sea presented the slightest attraction to him. He loved to lie in the very centre of five millions of people, with his filaments stretching out and running through them, responsive to every little rumour or suspicion of unsolved crime. Appreciation of Nature found no place among his many gifts, and his only change was when he turned his mind from the evil doer of the town to track down his brother of the country.

Finding that Holmes was too absorbed for conversation, I had tossed aside the barren paper, and, leaning back in my chair, I fell into a brown study. Suddenly my companion's voice broke in upon my thoughts.

'You are right, Watson,' said he. 'It does seem a very preposterous way of settling a dispute.'

'Most preposterous!' I exclaimed, and then suddenly realizing how he had echoed the inmost thought of my soul, I sat up in my chair and stared at him in blank amazement.

'What is this, Holmes?' I cried. 'This is beyond anything which I could have imagined.'

He laughed heartily at my perplexity.

'You remember,' said he, 'that some little time ago when I read you a passage in one of Poe's sketches, in which a close reasoner follows the unspoken thoughts of his companion, you were inclined to treat the matter as a mere *tour de force* of the author. On my remarking that I was constantly in the habit of doing the same thing you expressed incredulity.'

'Oh, no!'

'Perhaps not with your tongue, my dear Watson, but certainly with your eyebrows. So when I saw you throw down your paper and enter upon a train of thought, I was very happy to have the opportunity of reading it off, and eventually of breaking into it, as a proof that I had been *en rapport* with you.'

But I was still far from satisfied. 'In the example which you read to me,' said I, 'the reasoner drew his conclusions from the actions of the man whom he observed. If I remember right, he stumbled over a heap of stones, looked up at the stars, and so on. But I have been seated quietly in my chair, and what clues can I have given you?'

'You do yourself an injustice. The features are given to man as the means by which he shall express his emotions, and yours are faithful servants.'

'Do you mean to say that you read my train of thoughts from my features?'

'Your features, and especially your eyes. Perhaps you cannot yourself recall how your reverie commenced?'

'No, I cannot.'

'Then I will tell you. After throwing down your paper, which was the action which drew my attention to you, you sat for half a minute with a vacant expression. Then your eyes fixed themselves upon your newly framed picture of General Gordon, and I saw by the alteration in your face that a train of thought had been started. But it did not lead very far. Your eyes turned across to the unframed portrait of Henry Ward Beecher which stands upon the top of your books. You then glanced up at the wall, and of course your meaning was obvious. You were thinking that if the portrait were framed, it would just cover that bare space and correspond with Gordon's picture over there.'

'You have followed me wonderfully!' I exclaimed.

'So far I could hardly have gone astray. But

now your thoughts went back to Beecher, and you looked hard across as if you were studying the character in his features. Then your eyes ceased to pucker, but you continued to look across, and your face was thoughtful. You were recalling the incidents of Beecher's career. I was well aware that you could not do this without thinking of the mission which he undertook on behalf of the North at the time of the Civil War, for I remember your expressing your passionate indignation at the way in which he was received by the more turbulent of our people. You felt so strongly about it, that I knew you could not think of Beecher without thinking of that also. When a moment later I saw your eyes wander away from the picture, I suspected that your mind had now turned to the Civil War, and when I observed that your lips set, your eyes sparkled, and your hands clenched, I was positive that you were indeed thinking of the gallantry which was shown by both sides in that desperate struggle. But then, again, your face grew sadder; you shook your head. You were dwelling upon the sadness and horror and useless waste of life. Your hand stole towards your own old wound and a smile quivered on your lips, which showed me that the ridiculous side of this method of settling international questions had forced itself upon your mind. At this point I agreed with you that it was preposterous, and was glad to find that all my deductions had been correct.'

'Absolutely!' said I. 'And now that you have

explained it, I confess that I am as amazed as before.'

'It was very superficial, my dear Watson, I assure you. I should have not intruded it upon your attention had you not shown some incredulity the other day. But the evening has brought a breeze with it. What do you say to a ramble through London?'

I was weary of our little sitting-room, and gladly acquiesced. For three hours we strolled about together, watching the everchanging kaleidoscope of life as it ebbs and flows through Fleet Street and the Strand. Holmes's characteristic talk, with its keen observance of detail and subtle power of inference, held me amused and enthralled.

It was ten o'clock before we reached Baker Street again. A brougham was waiting at our door.

'Hum! A doctor's – general practitioner, I perceive,' said Holmes. 'Not been long in practice, but has had a good deal to do. Come to consult us, I fancy! Lucky we came back!'

I was sufficiently conversant with Holmes's methods to be able to follow his reasoning, and to see that the nature and state of the various medical instruments in the wicker basket which hung in the lamp-light inside the brougham had given him the data for his swift deduction. The light in our window above showed that this late visit was indeed intended for us. With some curiosity as to what could have sent a brother medico to us at such an hour, I followed Holmes into our sanctum.

A pale, taper-faced man with sandy whiskers rose up from a chair by the fire as we entered. His age may not have been more than three or four and thirty, but his haggard expression and unhealthy hue told of a life which had sapped his strength and robbed him of his youth. His manner was nervous and shy, like that of a sensitive gentleman, and the thin white hand which he laid on the mantelpiece as he rose was that of an artist rather than of a surgeon. His dress was quiet and sombre, a black frock-coat, dark trousers, and a touch of colour about his necktie.

'Good evening, doctor,' said Holmes cheerily; 'I am glad to see that you have only been waiting a very few minutes.'

'You spoke to my coachman, then?'

'No, it was the candle on the side-table that told me. Pray resume your seat and let me know how I can serve you.'

'My name is Doctor Percy Trevelyan,' said our visitor, 'and I live at 403 Brook Street.'

'Are you not the author of a monograph upon obscure nervous lesions?' I asked.

His pale cheeks flushed with pleasure at hearing that his work was known to me.

'I so seldom hear of the work that I thought it was quite dead,' said he. 'My publishers give me a most discouraging account of its sale. You are yourself, I presume, a medical man?'

'A retired Army surgeon.'

'My own hobby has always been nervous disease. I should wish to make it an absolute speciality, but, of course, a man must take what he can get first. This, however, is beside the question, Mr Sherlock Holmes, and I quite appreciate how valuable your time is. The fact is that a very singular train of events has occurred recently at my house in Brook Street, and tonight they came to such a head that I felt it was quite impossible for me to wait another hour before asking for your advice and assistance.'

Sherlock Holmes sat down and lit his pipe. 'You are very welcome to both,' said he. 'Pray let me have a detailed account of what the circumstances are which have disturbed you.'

'One or two of them are so trivial,' said Dr Trevelyan, 'that really I am almost ashamed to mention them. But the matter is so inexplicable, and the recent turn which it has taken is so elaborate, that I shall lay it all before you, and you shall judge what is essential and what is not.

'I am compelled, to begin with, to say something of my own college career. I am a London University man, you know, and I am sure you will not think that I am unduly singing my own praises if I say that my student career was considered by my professors to be a very promising one. After I had graduated I continued to devote myself to research, occupying a minor position in King's College Hospital, and I was fortunate enough to excite considerable interest by my research into the pathology of catalepsy, and finally to win the Bruce Pinkerton prize and medal by the monograph on nervous lesions to which your friend has just alluded. I should not go too far if I were to say that there was a general impression at that time that a distinguished career lay before me.

'But the one great stumbling-block lay in my want of capital. As you will readily understand, a specialist who aims high is compelled to start in one of a dozen streets in the Cavendish Square quarter, all of which entail enormous rents and furnishing expenses. Besides this preliminary outlay, he must be prepared to keep himself for some years, and to hire a presentable carriage and horse. To do this was quite beyond my power, and I could only hope that by economy I might in ten years' time save enough to enable me to put up my plate. Suddenly, however, an unexpected incident opened up quite a new prospect to me.

'This was a visit from a gentleman of the name of Blessington, who was a complete stranger to me. He came up into my room one morning, and plunged into business in an instant.

'"You are the same Percy Trevelyan who has had so distinguished a career and won a great prize lately?" said he.

'I bowed.

'"Answer me frankly," he continued, "for you will find it to your interest to do so. You have all the cleverness which makes a successful man. Have you the tact?"

'I could not help but smile at the abruptness of the question.

'"I trust that I have my share," I said.

'"Any bad habits? Not drawn towards drink, eh?"

'"Really, sir!" I cried.

'"Quite right! That's all right! But I was bound to ask. With all these qualities why are you not in practice?"

'I shrugged my shoulders.

'"Come, come!" said he, in his bustling way. "It's the old story. More in your brains than in your pocket, eh? What would you say if I were to start you in Brook Street?"

'I stared at him in astonishment.

'"Oh, it's for my sake, not for yours," he cried. "I'll be perfectly frank with you, and if it suits you it will suit me very well. I have a few thousands to invest, d'ye see, and I think I'll sink them in you."

'"But why?" I gasped.

'"Well, it's just like any other speculation, and safer than most."

'"What am I to do, then?"

'"I'll tell you. I'll take the house, furnish it, pay the maids, and run the whole place. All you have to do is to wear out your chair in the consulting-room. I'll let you have pocket money and everything. Then you hand over to me three-quarters of what you earn, and you keep the other quarter for yourself."

'This was the strange proposal, Mr Holmes, with which the man Blessington approached me. I won't weary you with the account of how we bargained and negotiated. It ended in my moving into the house next Lady Day, and starting in practice on very much the same conditions as he had suggested. He came himself to live with me in the character of a resident patient. His heart was weak, it appears, and he needed constant medical supervision. He turned the two best rooms on the first floor into a sitting-room and bedroom for himself. He was a man of singular habits, shunning company and very seldom going out. His life was irregular, but in one respect he was regularity itself. Every evening at the same hour he walked into the consulting-room, examined the books, put down five and threepence for every guinea that I had earned, and carried the rest off to the strong-box in his own room.

'I may say with confidence that he never had occasion to regret his speculation. From the first it was a success. A few good cases and the reputation which I had won in the hospital brought me rapidly to the front, and during the last year or two I have made him a rich man.

'So much, Mr Holmes, for my past history and my relations with Mr Blessington. It only remains for me now to tell you what has occurred to bring me here tonight.

'Some weeks ago Mr Blessington came down to me in, as it seemed to me, a state of considerable agitation. He spoke of some burglary which, he said, had been committed in the West End, and he appeared, I remember, to be quite unnecessarily excited about it, declaring that a day should not pass before we should add stronger bolts to our windows and doors. For a week he continued to be in a peculiar state of restlessness, peering continually out of the windows, and ceasing to take the short walk which had usually been the prelude to his dinner. From his manner it struck me that he was in mortal dread of something or somebody, but when I questioned him upon the point he became so offensive that I was compelled to drop the subject. Gradually as time passed his fears appeared to die away, and he had renewed his former habits, when a fresh event reduced him to the pitiable state of prostration in which he now lies.

'What happened was this. Two days ago I received the letter which I now read to you. Neither address nor date is attached to it.

'"A Russian nobleman who is now resident in England," it runs, "would be glad to avail himself of the professional assistance of Dr Percy Trevelyan. He has been for some years a victim to cataleptic attacks, on which, as is well known, Dr Trevelyan is an authority. He proposes to call at about a quarter past six tomorrow evening, if Dr Trevelyan will make it convenient to be at home."

'This letter interested me deeply, because the chief difficulty in the study of catalepsy is the rareness of the disease. You may believe, then, that I was in my consulting-room when, at the appointed hour, the page showed in the patient.

'He was an elderly man, thin, demure, and commonplace – by no means the conception one forms of a Russian nobleman. I was much more struck by the appearance of his companion. This was a tall young man, surprisingly handsome, with a dark, fierce face, and the limbs and chest of a Hercules. He had his hand under the other's arm as they entered, and helped him to a chair with a tenderness which one would hardly have expected from his appearance.

'"You will excuse my coming in, doctor," said he to me, speaking English with a slight lisp. "This is my father, and his health is a matter of the most overwhelming importance to me."

'I was touched by his filial anxiety. "You would, perhaps, care to remain during the consultation?" said I.

'"Not for the world," he cried, with a gesture of horror. "It is more painful to me that I can express. If I were to see my father in one of those dreadful seizures, I am convinced that I should never survive it. My own nervous system is an exceptionally sensitive one. With your permission I will remain in the waiting-room while you go into my father's case."

'To this, of course, I assented, and the young

man withdrew. The patient and I then plunged into a discussion of his case, of which I took exhaustive notes. He was not remarkable for intelligence, and his answers were frequently obscure, which I attributed to his limited acquaintance with our language. Suddenly, however, as I sat writing he ceased to give any answer at all to my inquiries, and on my turning towards him I was shocked to see that he was sitting bolt upright in his chair, staring at me with a perfectly blank and rigid face. He was again in the grip of his mysterious malady.

'My first feeling, as I have just said, was one of pity and horror. My second, I fear, was rather one of professional satisfaction. I made notes of my patient's pulse and temperature, tested the rigidity of his muscles, and examined his reflexes. There was nothing markedly abnormal in any of these conditions, which harmonized with my former experiences. I had obtained good results in such cases by the inhalation of nitrate of amyl, and the present seemed an admirable opportunity of testing its virtues. The bottle was downstairs in my laboratory, so, leaving my patient seated in his chair, I ran down to get it. There was some little delay in finding it – five minutes, let us say – and then I returned. Imagine my amazement to find the room empty and the patient gone!

'Of course, my first act was to run into the waiting-room. The son had gone also. The hall door had been closed, but not shut. My page who admits patients is a new boy, and by no means quick. He waits downstairs, and runs up to show patients out when I ring the consulting-room bell. He had heard nothing, and the affair remained a complete mystery. Mr Blessington came in from his walk shortly afterwards, but I did not say anything to him upon the subject, for to tell the truth, I have got in the way of late of holding as little communication with him as possible.

'Well, I never thought that I should see anything more of the Russian and his son, so you can imagine my amazement when at the very same hour this evening they both came marching into my consulting-room, just as they had done before.

'"I feel that I owe you a great many apologies for my abrupt departure yesterday, Doctor," said my patient.

'"I confess that I was very much surprised at it," said I.

'"Well, the fact is," he remarked, "that when I recover from these attacks my mind is always very clouded as to all that has gone before. I woke up in a strange room, as it seemed to me, and made my way out into the street in a sort of dazed way when you were absent."

'"And I," said the son, "seeing my father pass the door of the waiting-room, naturally thought that the consultation had come to an end. It was not until we had reached home that I began to realize the true state of affairs."

'"Well," said I, laughing, "there is no harm

done, except that you puzzled me terribly; so if you, sir, would kindly step into the waiting-room, I shall be happy to continue our consultation, which was brought to so abrupt an ending.''

'For half an hour or so I discussed the old gentleman's symptoms with him, and then, having prescribed for him, I saw him go off on the arm of his son.

'I have told you that Mr Blessington generally chose this hour of the day for his exercise. He came in shortly afterwards and passed upstairs. An instant later I heard him running down, and he burst into my consulting-room like a man who is mad with panic.

' ''Who has been in my room?'' he cried.

' ''No one,'' said I.

' ''It's a lie!'' he yelled. ''Come up and look.''

'I passed over the grossness of his language, as he seemed half out of his mind with fear. When I went upstairs with him he pointed to several footprints upon the light carpet.

' ''D'you mean to say those are mine?'' he cried.

'They were certainly very much larger than any which he could have made, and were evidently quite fresh. It rained hard this afternoon, as you know, and my patients were the only people who called. It must have been the case, then, that the man in the waiting-room had for some unknown reason, while I was busy with the other, ascended to the room of my resident patient. Nothing had been touched or taken, but there were the foot-prints to prove that the intrusion was a undoubted fact.

'Mr Blessington seemed more excited over the matter than I should have thought possible, though, of course, it was enough to disturb any-body's peace of mind. He actually sat crying in an armchair, and I could hardly get him to speak coherently. It was his suggestion that I should come round to you, and of course I at once saw the propriety of it, for certainly the incident is a very singular one, though he appears to completely overrate its importance. If you would only come back with me in my brougham, you would at least be able to soothe him, though I can hardly hope that you will be able to explain this remarkable occurrence.'

Sherlock Holmes had listened to this long narra-tive with an intentness which showed me that his interest was keenly aroused. His face was as impas-sive as ever, but his lids had dropped more heavily over his eyes, and his smoke had curled up more thickly from his pipe to emphasize each curious episode in the doctor's tale. As our visitor con-cluded Holmes sprang up without a word, handed me my hat, picked up his own from the table, and followed Dr Trevelyan to the door. Within a quar-ter of an hour we had been dropped at the door of the physician's residence in Brook Street, one of those sombre, flat-faced houses which one asso-ciates with a West End practice. A small page admitted us, and we began at once to ascend the broad, well-carpeted stair.

But a singular interruption brought us to a standstill. The light at the top was suddenly whisked out, and from the darkness came a reedy, quavering voice.

'I have a pistol,' it cried; 'I give you my word that I'll fire if you come any nearer.'

'This really grows outrageous, Mr Blessington,' cried Dr Trevelyan.

'Oh, then it is you, Doctor?' said the voice, with a great heave of relief. 'But those other gentlemen, are they what they pretend to be?'

We were conscious of a long scrutiny out of the darkness.

'Yes, yes, it's all right,' said the voice at last. 'You can come up, and I am sorry if my precautions have annoyed you.'

He re-lit the stair gas as he spoke, and we saw before us a singular-looking man, whose appearance, as well as his voice, testified to his jangled nerves. He was very fat, but had apparently at some time been much fatter, so that the skin hung about his face in loose pouches, like the cheeks of a bloodhound. He was of a sickly colour, and his thin, sandy hair seemed to bristle up with the intensity of his emotion. In his hand he held a pistol, but he thrust it into his pocket as we advanced.

'Good evening, Mr Holmes,' said he; 'I am sure I am very much obliged to you for coming round.

No one ever needed your advice more than I do. I suppose that Dr Trevelyan has told you of this most unwarrantable intrusion into my rooms?'

'Quite so,' said Holmes. 'Who are these two men, Mr Blessington, and why do they wish to molest you?'

'Well, well,' said the resident patient, in a nervous fashion, 'of course it is hard to say that. You can hardly expect me to answer that, Mr Holmes.'

'Do you mean that you don't know?'

'Come in here, if you please. Just have the kindness to step in here.'

He led the way into his bedroom, which was large and comfortably furnished.

'You see that?' said he, pointing to a big black box at the end of his bed. 'I have never been a very rich man, Mr Holmes – never made but one investment in my life, as Dr Trevelyan would tell you. But I don't believe in bankers. I would never trust a banker, Mr Holmes. Between ourselves, what little I have is in that box, so you can understand what it means to me when unknown people force themselves into my rooms.'

Holmes looked at Blessington in his questioning way, and shook his head.

'I cannot possibly advise you if you try to deceive me,' said he.

'But I have told you everything.'

Holmes turned on his heel with a gesture of disgust. 'Good night, Dr Trevelyan,' said he.

'And no advice for me?' cried Blessington, in a breaking voice.

'My advice to you, sir, is to speak the truth.'

A minute later we were in the street and walking for home. We had crossed Oxford Street, and were half-way down Harley Street before I could get a word from my companion.

'Sorry to bring you out on such a fool's errand, Watson,' he said, at last. 'It is an interesting case, too, at the bottom of it.'

'I can make little of it,' I confessed.

'Well, it is quite evident that there are two men – more, perhaps, but at least two – who are determined for some reason to get at this fellow, Blessington. I have no doubt in my mind that both on the first and on the second occasion that young man penetrated to Blessington's room, while his confederate, by an ingenious device, kept the doctor from interfering.'

'And the catalepsy!'

'A fraudulent imitation, Watson, though I should hardly dare to hint as much to our specialist. It is a very easy complaint to imitate. I have done it myself.'

'And then?'

'By the purest chance Blessington was out on each occasion. Their reason for choosing so unusual an hour for a consultation was obviously to ensure that there should be no other patient in the waiting-room. It just happened, however, that this hour coincided with Blessington's constitutional, which seems to show that they were not very well acquainted with his daily routine. Of course, if they had been merely after plunder they would at least have made some attempt to search for it. Besides, I can read in a man's eye when it is his own skin that he is frightened for. It is inconceivable that this fellow could have made two such vindictive enemies as these appear to be without knowing of it. I hold it, therefore, to be certain that he does know who these men are, and that for reasons of his own he suppresses it. It is just possible that tomorrow may find him in a more communicative mood.'

'Is there not one alternative,' I suggested, 'grotesquely improbable, no doubt, but still just conceivable? Might the whole story of the cataleptic Russian and his son be a concoction of Dr Trevelyan's, who has, for his own purposes, been in Blessington's rooms?'

I saw in the gaslight that Holmes wore an amused smile at this brilliant departure of mine.

'My dear fellow,' said he, 'it was one of the first solutions which occurred to me, but I was soon able to corroborate the doctor's tale. This young man has left prints upon the stair carpet which made it quite superfluous for me to ask to see those which he had made in the room. When I tell you that his shoes were square-toed, instead of being pointed like Blessington's, and were quite an inch and a third longer than the doctor's, you will acknowledge that there can be no doubt as to his individuality. But we may sleep on it now, for I shall be surprised if we do not hear something further from Brook Street in the morning.'

Sherlock Holmes's prophecy was soon fulfilled, and in a dramatic fashion. At half past seven next morning, in the first glimmer of daylight, I found him standing by my bedside in his dressing-gown.

'There's a brougham waiting for us, Watson,' said he.

'What's the matter, then?'

'The Brook Street business.'

'Any fresh news?'

'Tragic, but ambiguous,' said he, pulling up the blind. 'Look at this – a sheet from a note-book with "For God's sake, come at once – P.T." scrawled upon it in pencil. Our friend the doctor was hard put to it when he wrote this. Come along, my dear fellow, for it's an urgent call.'

In a quarter of an hour or so we were back at the physician's house. He came running out to meet us with a face of horror.

'Oh, such a business!' he cried, with his hands to his temples.

'What, then?'

'Blessington has committed suicide!'

Holmes whistled.

'Yes, he hanged himself during the night!'

We had entered, and the doctor had preceded us into what was evidently his waiting-room.

'I really hardly know what I am doing,' he

cried. 'The police are already upstairs. It has shaken me most dreadfully.'

'When did you find it out?'

'He has a cup of tea taken to him early every morning. When the maid entered about seven, there the unfortunate fellow was hanging in the middle of the room. He had tied his cord to the hook on which the heavy lamp used to hang, and he had jumped off from the top of the very box that he showed us yesterday.'

Holmes stood for a moment in deep thought.

'With your permission,' said he at last, 'I should like to go upstairs and look into the matter.' We both ascended, followed by the doctor.

It was a dreadful sight which met us as we entered the bedroom door. I have spoken of the impression of flabbiness which this man Blessington conveyed. As he dangled from the hook it was exaggerated and intensified until he was scarce human in his appearance. The neck was drawn out like a plucked chicken's, making the rest of him seem the more obese and unnatural by the contrast. He was clad only in his long night-dress, and his swollen ankles and ungainly feet protruded starkly from beneath it. Beside him stood a smart-looking police inspector, who was taking notes in a pocket-book.

'Ah, Mr Holmes,' said he, as my friend entered. 'I am delighted to see you.'

'Good morning, Lanner,' answered Holmes. 'You won't think me an intruder, I am sure. Have you heard of the events which led up to this affair?'

'Yes, I heard something of them.'

'Have you formed any opinion?'

'As far as I can see, the man has been driven out of his senses by fright. The bed has been well slept in, you see. There's his impression deep enough. It's about five in the morning, you know, that suicides are most common. That would be about his time for hanging himself. It seems to have been a very deliberate affair.'

'I should say that he has been dead about three hours, judging by the rigidity of the muscles,' said I.

'Noticed anything peculiar about the room?' asked Holmes.

'Found a screwdriver and some screws on the wash-hand stand. Seems to have smoked heavily during the night, too. Here are four cigar ends that I picked out of the fireplace.'

'Hum!' said Holmes. 'Have you got his cigar-holder?'

'No, I have seen none.'

'His cigar-case, then?'

'Yes, it was in his coat-pocket.'

Holmes opened it and smelled the single cigar which it contained.

'Oh, this is a Havana, and these others are cigars of the peculiar sort which are imported by the Dutch from their East Indian Colonies. They are usually wrapped in straw, you know, and are thinner for their length than any other brand.' He picked up the four ends and examined them with his pocket lens.

'Two of these have been smoked from a holder and two without,' said he. 'Two have been cut by a not very sharp knife, and two have had the ends bitten off by a set of excellent teeth. This is no suicide, Mr Lanner. It is a very deeply planned and cold-blooded murder.'

'Impossible!' cried the inspector.

'And why?'

'Why should anyone murder a man in so clumsy a fashion as by hanging him?'

'That is what we have to find out.'

'How could they get in?'

'Through the front door.'

'It was barred in the morning.'

'Then it was barred after them.'

'How do you know?'

'I saw their traces. Excuse me a moment, and I may be able to give you some further information about it.'

He went over to the door, and turning the lock he examined it in his methodical fashion. Then he took out the key, which was on the inside, and inspected that also. The bed, the carpet, the chairs, the mantelpiece, the dead body, and the rope were each in turn examined, until at last he professed himself satisfied, and with my aid and that of the inspector cut down the wretched object, and laid it reverently under a sheet.

'How about this rope?' he asked.

'It is cut off this,' said Dr Trevelyan, drawing a large coil from under the bed. 'He was morbidly nervous of fire, and always kept this beside him, so that he might escape by the window in case the stairs were burning.'

'That must have saved them trouble,' said Holmes thoughtfully. 'Yes, the actual facts are very plain, and I shall be surprised if by the afternoon I cannot give you the reasons for them as well. I will take this photograph of Blessington which I see upon the mantelpiece, as it may help me in my inquiries.'

'But you have told us nothing,' cried the doctor.

'Oh, there can be no doubt as to the sequence of events,' said Holmes. 'There were three of them in it: the young man, the old man, and a third to whose identity I have no clue. The first two, I need hardly remark, are the same who masqueraded as the Russian Count and his son, so we can give a very full description of them. They were admitted by a confederate inside the house. If I might offer you a word of advice, Inspector, it would be to arrest the page, who, as I understand, has only recently come into your service, Doctor.'

'The young imp cannot be found,' said Dr Trevelyan; 'the maid and the cook have just been searching for him.'

Holmes shrugged his shoulders.

'He has played a not unimportant part in this drama.' said he. 'The three men having ascended the stair, which they did on tiptoe, the elder man first, the younger man second, and the unknown man in the rear –'

'My dear Holmes!' I ejaculated.

'Oh, there could be no question as to the super-imposing of the footmarks. I had the advantage of learning which was which last night. They ascended then to Mr Blessington's room, the door of which they found to be locked. With the help of a wire, however, they forced round the key. Even without the lens, you will perceive, by the scratches on this ward, where the pressure was applied.

'On entering the room, their first proceeding must have been to gag Mr Blessington. He may have been asleep, or he may have been so paralysed with terror as to have been unable to cry out. These walls are thick, and it is conceivable that his shriek, if he had time to utter one, was unheard.

'Having secured him, it is evident to me that a consultation of some sort was held. Probably it was something in the nature of a judicial proceeding. It must have lasted for some time, for it was then that these cigars were smoked. The older man sat in that wicker chair: it was he who used the cigar-holder. The younger man sat over yonder; he knocked his ash off against the chest of drawers. The third fellow paced up and down.

Blessington, I think, sat upright in the bed, but of that I cannot be absolutely certain.

'Well, it ended by their taking Blessington and hanging him. The matter was so pre-arranged that it is my belief that they brought with them some sort of block or pulley which might serve as a gallows. That screwdriver and those screws were, as I conceive, for fixing it up. Seeing the hook, however, they naturally saved themselves the trouble. Having finished their work they made off, and the door was barred behind them by their confederate.'

We had all listened with the deepest interest to this sketch of the night's doings, which Holmes had deduced from signs so subtle and minute, that even when he had pointed them out to us, we could scarcely follow him in his reasonings. The inspector hurried away on the instant to make inquiries about the page, while Holmes and I returned to Baker Street for breakfast.

'I'll be back by three,' said he when we had finished our meal. 'Both the inspector and the doctor will meet me here at that hour, and I hope by that time to have cleared up any little obscurity which the case may still present.'

Our visitors arrived at the appointed time, but it was a quarter to four before my friend put in an appearance. From his expression as he entered, however, I could see that all had gone well with him.

'Any news, Inspector?'

'We have got the boy, sir.'

'Excellent, and I have got the men.'

'You have got them!' we cried all three.

'Well, at least I have got their identity. This so-called Blessington is, as I expected, well known at headquarters, and so are his assailants. Their names are Biddle, Hayward, and Moffat.'

'The Worthingdon bank gang,' cried the inspector.

'Precisely,' said Holmes.

'Then Blessington must have been Sutton?'

'Exactly,' said Holmes.

'Why, that makes it as clear as crystal,' said the inspector.

But Trevelyan and I looked at each other in bewilderment.

'You must surely remember the great Worthingdon bank business,' said Holmes; 'five men were in it, these four and a fifth called Cartwright. Tobin, the caretaker, was murdered, and the thieves got away with seven thousand pounds. This was in 1875. They were all five arrested, but the evidence against them was by no means conclusive. This Blessington or Sutton, who was the worst of the gang, turned informer. On his evidence Cartwright was hanged, and the other three got fifteen years apiece. When they got out the other day, which was some years before their full term, they set themselves, as you perceive, to hunt down the traitor and to avenge the death of their comrade upon him. Twice they tried to get at him and failed; a third time, you see, it came off. Is there anything further which I can explain, Dr Trevelyan?'

'I think you have made it all remarkably clear,' said the doctor. 'No doubt the day on which he was so perturbed was the day when he read of their release in the newspapers.'

'Quite so. His talk about a burglary was the merest blind.'

'But why could he not tell you this?'

'Well, my dear sir, knowing the vindictive character of his old associates, he was trying to hide his own identity from everybody as long as he could. His secret was a shameful one, and he could not bring himself to divulge it. However, wretch as he was, he was still living under the shield of British law, and I have no doubt, Inspector, that you will see that, though that shield may fail to guard, the sword of justice is still there to avenge.'

Such were the singular circumstances in connexion with the resident patient and the Brook Street doctor. From that night nothing has been seen of the three murderers by the police, and it is surmised at Scotland Yard that they were among the passengers of the ill-fated steamer *Norah Creina*, which was lost some years ago with all hands upon the Portuguese coast, some leagues to the north of Oporto. The proceedings against the page broke down for want of evidence, and the 'Brook Street Mystery', as it was called, has never, until now, been fully dealt with in any public print.

We were seated at breakfast one morning, my wife and I, when the maid brought in a telegram. It was from Sherlock Holmes, and ran in this way:

'Have you a couple of days to spare? Have just been wired for from the West of England in connection with Boscombe Valley tragedy. Shall be glad if you will come with me. Air and scenery perfect. Leave Paddington by the 11.15.'

'What do you say, dear?' said my wife, looking across at me. 'Will you go?'

'I really don't know what to say. I have a fairly long list at present.'

'Oh, Anstruther would do your work for you. You have been looking a little pale lately. I think that the change would do you good, and you are always so interested in Mr Sherlock Holmes's cases.'

'I should be ungrateful if I were not, seeing what I gained through one of them,' I answered. 'But if I am to go I must pack at once, for I have only half an hour.'

My experience of camp life in Afghanistan had at least had the effect of making me a prompt and ready traveller. My wants were few and simple, so that in less than the time stated I was in a cab with my valise, rattling away to Paddington Station. Sherlock Holmes was pacing up and down the platform, his tall, gaunt figure made even gaunter and taller by his long grey travelling-cloak and close-fitting cloth cap.

'It is really very good of you to come, Watson,' said he. 'It makes a considerable difference to me, having someone with me on whom I can thoroughly rely. Local aid is always either worthless or else biased. If you will keep the two corner seats I shall get the tickets.'

We had the carriage to ourselves save for an immense litter of papers which Holmes had brought with him. Among these he rummaged and read, with intervals of note-taking and of meditation, until we were past Reading. Then he suddenly rolled them all into a gigantic ball, and tossed them up on to the rack.

'Have you heard anything of the case?' he asked.

'Not a word. I have not seen a paper for some days.'

'The London press has not had very full accounts. I have just been looking through all the recent papers in order to master the particulars. It seems, from what I gather, to be one of those simple cases which are so extremely difficult.'

'That sounds a little paradoxical.'

'But it is profoundly true. Singularity is almost

invariably a clue. The more featureless and commonplace a crime is, the more difficult it is to
bring it home. In this case, however, they have
established a very serious case against the son of
the murdered man.'

'It is a murder, then?'

'Well, it is conjectured to be so. I shall take
nothing for granted until I have the opportunity
of looking personally into it. I will explain the
state of things to you, as far as I have been able to
understand it, in a very few words.

'Boscombe Valley is a country district not very
far from Ross, in Herefordshire. The largest
landed proprietor in that part is a Mr John
Turner, who made his money in Australia, and
returned some years ago to the old country. One
of the farms which he held, that of Hatherley, was
let to Mr Charles McCarthy, who was also an ex-
Australian. The men had known each other in the
Colonies, so that it was not unnatural that when
they came to settle down they should do so as
near each other as possible. Turner was apparently
the richer man, so McCarthy became his tenant,
but still remained, it seems, upon terms of perfect
equality, as they were frequently together. McCarthy had one son, a lad of eighteen, and Turner
had an only daughter of the same age, but neither
of them had wives living. They appear to have
avoided the society of the neighbouring English
families, and to have led retired lives, though both
the McCarthys were fond of sport, and were

frequently seen at the race meetings of the neigh-bourhood. McCarthy kept two servants – a man and a girl. Turner had a considerable household, some half dozen at the least. That is as much as I have been able to gather about the families. Now for the facts.

'On June 3 – that is, on Monday last – McCar-thy left his house at Hatherley about three in the afternoon, and walked down to the Boscombe Pool, which is a small lake formed by the spread-ing out of the stream which runs down the Boscombe Valley. He had been out with his serving-man in the morning at Ross, and he had told the man that he must hurry, as he had an appointment of importance to keep at three. From that appointment he never came back alive.

'From Hatherley Farm-house to the Boscombe Pool is a quarter of a mile, and two people saw him as he passed over this ground. One was an old woman, whose name is not mentioned, and the other was William Crowder, a gamekeeper in the employ of Mr Turner. Both these witnesses depose that Mr McCarthy was walking alone. The gamekeeper adds that within a few minutes of his seeing Mr McCarthy pass he had seen his son, Mr James McCarthy, going the same way with a gun under his arm. To the best of his belief, the father was actually in sight at the time, and the son was following him. He thought no more of the matter until he heard in the evening of the tragedy that had occurred.

'The two McCarthys were seen after the time when William Crowder, the gamekeeper, lost sight of them. The Boscombe Pool is thickly wooded round, with just a fringe of grass and of reeds round the edge. A girl of fourteen, Patience Moran, who is the daughter of the lodge-keeper of the Boscombe Valley Estate, was in one of the woods picking flowers. She states that while she was there she saw, at the border of the wood and close by the lake, Mr McCarthy and his son, and that they appeared to be having a violent quarrel. She heard Mr McCarthy the elder using very strong language to his son, and she saw the latter raise up his hand as if to strike his father. She was so frightened by their violence that she ran away, and told her mother when she reached home that she had left the two McCarthys quarrelling near Boscombe Pool, and that she was afraid that they were going to fight. She had hardly said the words when young Mr McCarthy came running up to the lodge to say that he had found his father dead in the wood, and to ask for the help of the lodge-keeper. He was much excited, without either his gun or his hat, and his right hand and sleeve were observed to be stained with fresh blood. On following him they found the dead body of his father stretched out upon the grass beside the Pool. The head had been beaten in by repeated blows of some heavy and blunt weapon. The injuries were such as might very well have been inflicted by the butt-end of his son's gun, which was found lying on the grass within a few paces of the body. Under these circumstances the young man was instantly arrested, and a verdict of "Wilful Murder" having been returned at the inquest on Tuesday, he was on Wednesday brought before the magistrates at Ross, who have referred the case to the next assizes. Those are the main facts of the case as they came out before the coroner and at the police-court.'

'I could hardly imagine a more damning case,' I remarked. 'If ever circumstantial evidence pointed to a criminal it does so here.'

'Circumstantial evidence is a very tricky thing,' answered Holmes thoughtfully; 'it may seem to point very straight to one thing, but if you shift your own point of view a little, you may find it pointing in an equally uncompromising manner to something entirely different. It must be confessed, however, that the case looks exceedingly grave against the young man, and it is very possible that he is indeed the culprit. There are several people in the neighbourhood, however, and among them Miss Turner, the daughter of the neighbouring landowner, who believe in his innocence, and who have retained Lestrade, whom you may remember in connection with the Study in Scarlet, to work out the case in his interest. Lestrade, being rather puzzled, has referred the case to me, and hence it is that two middle-aged gentlemen are flying westward at fifty miles an hour, instead of quietly digesting their breakfasts at home.'

'I am afraid,' said I, 'that the facts are so obvious that you will find little credit to be gained out of this case.'

'There is nothing more deceptive than an obvious fact,' he answered, laughing. 'Besides, we may chance to hit upon some other obvious facts which may have been by no means obvious to Mr Lestrade. You know me too well to think that I am boasting when I say that I shall either confirm or destroy his theory by means which he is quite incapable of employing, or even of understanding. To take the first example to hand, I very clearly perceive that in your bedroom the window is upon the righthand side, and yet I question whether Mr Lestrade would have noted even so self-evident a thing as that.'

'How on earth –!'

'My dear fellow, I know you well. I know the military neatness which characterizes you. You shave every morning, and in this season you shave by the sunlight, but since your shaving is less and less complete as we get farther back on the left side, until it becomes positively slovenly as we get round the angle of the jaw, it is surely very clear that that side is less well illuminated than the other. I could not imagine a man of your habits looking at himself in an equal light, and being satisfied with such a result. I only quote this as a trivial example of observation and inference. Therein lies my *métier*, and it is just possible that it may be of some service in the investigation which lies before us. There are one or two minor points which were brought out in the inquest, and which are worth considering.'

'What are they?'

'It appears that his arrest did not take place at once, but after the return to Hatherley Farm. On the inspector of constabulary informing him that he was a prisoner, he remarked that he was not surprised to hear it, and that it was no more than his deserts. This observation of his had the natural effect of removing any traces of doubt which might have remained in the minds of the coroner's jury.'

'It was a confession,' I ejaculated.

'No, for it was followed by a protestation of innocence.'

'Coming on the top of such a damning series of events, it was at least a most suspicious remark.'

'On the contrary,' said Holmes, 'it is the brightest rift which I can at present see in the clouds. However innocent he might be, he could not be such an absolute imbecile as not to see that the circumstances were very black against him. Had he appeared surprised at his own arrest, or feigned indignation at it, I should have looked upon it as highly suspicious, because such surprise or anger would not be natural under the circumstances, and yet might appear to be the best policy to a scheming man. His frank acceptance of the situation marks him as either an innocent man, or else as a man of considerable self-restraint and firmness. As to his remark about his deserts, it was also not unnatural if you consider that he stood by the dead body of his father, and that there is no doubt that he had that very day so far forgotten his filial duty as to bandy words with him, and even, according to the little girl whose evidence is so important, to raise his hand as if to strike him. The self-reproach and contrition which are displayed in his remark appear to me to be the signs of a healthy mind, rather than of a guilty one.'

I shook my head. 'Many men have been hanged on far slighter evidence,' I remarked.

'So they have. And many men have been wrongfully hanged.'

'What is the young man's own account of the matter?'

'It is, I am afraid, not very encouraging to his supporters, though there are one or two points in it which are suggestive. You will find it here, and may read it for yourself.'

He picked out from his bundle a copy of the local Herefordshire paper, and having turned down the sheet, he pointed out the paragraph in which the unfortunate young man had given his own statement of what had occurred. I settled myself down in the corner of the carriage, and read it very carefully. It ran in this way:

Mr James McCarthy, the only son of the deceased, was then called, and gave evidence as follows: 'I had been away from home for three days at Bristol, and had only just returned upon the morning of last Monday, the 3rd. My father was absent from home at the time of my arrival, and I was informed by the maid that he had driven over to Ross with John Cobb, the groom. Shortly after my return I heard the wheels of his trap in the yard, and looking out of my window, I saw him get out and walk rapidly out of the yard, though I was not aware in which direction he was going. I then took my gun, and strolled out in the direction of the Boscombe Pool, with the intention of visiting the rabbit warren which is upon the other side. On my way I saw William Crowder, the game-keeper, as he has stated in his evidence; but he is mistaken in thinking that I was following my father. I had no idea that he was in front of me. When about a hundred yards from the Pool I heard a cry of "Cooee!" which was a usual signal between my father and myself. I then hurried forward, and found him standing by the Pool. He appeared to be much surprised at seeing me, and asked me rather roughly what I was doing there. A conversation ensued, which led to high words, and almost to blows, for my father was a man of a very violent temper. Seeing that his passion was becoming ungovernable, I left him, and returned towards Hatherley Farm. I had not gone more than one hundred and fifty yards, however, when I heard a hideous outcry behind me, which caused me to run back again. I found my father expiring on the ground, with his head terribly injured. I dropped my gun, and held him in my arms, but he almost instantly expired. I knelt beside him for some minutes, and then made my way to Mr Turner's lodge-keeper, his house being the nearest, to ask for assistance. I saw no one near my father when I returned, and I have no idea how he came by his injuries. He was not a popular man, being somewhat cold and forbidding in his manners; but he had, as far as I know, no active enemies. I know nothing further of the matter.'

The Coroner: Did your father make any statement to you before he died?

Witness: He mumbled a few words, but I could only catch some allusion to a rat.

The Coroner: What did you understand by that?

Witness: It conveyed no meaning to me. I thought that he was delirious.

The Coroner: What was the point upon which you and your father had this final quarrel?

Witness: I should prefer not to answer.

The Coroner: I am afraid that I must press it.

Witness: It is really impossible for me to tell you. I can assure you that it has nothing to do with the sad tragedy which followed.

The Coroner: That is for the Court to decide. I need not point out to you that your refusal to answer will prejudice your case considerably in any future proceedings which may arise.

Witness: I must still refuse.

The Coroner: I understand that the cry of

'Cooee' was a common signal between you and your father?

Witness: It was.

The Coroner: How was it, then, that he uttered it before he saw you, and before he even knew that you had returned from Bristol?

Witness (with considerable confusion): I do not know.

A Juryman: Did you see nothing which aroused your suspicions when you returned on hearing the cry, and found your father fatally injured?

Witness: Nothing definite.

The Coroner: What do you mean?

Witness: I was so disturbed and excited as I rushed out into the open, that I could think of nothing except my father. Yet I have a vague impression that as I ran forward something lay upon the ground to the left of me. It seemed to me to be something grey in colour, a coat of some sort, or a plaid perhaps. When I rose from my father I looked round for it, but it was gone.

Do you mean that it disappeared before you went for help?

Yes, it was gone.

You cannot say what it was?

No, I had a feeling something was there.

How far from the body?

A dozen yards or so.

And how far from the edge of the wood?

About the same.

Then if it was removed it was while you were within a dozen yards of it?

Yes, but with my back towards it.

This concluded the examination of the witness.

'I see,' said I, as I glanced down the column, 'that the coroner in his concluding remarks was rather severe upon young McCarthy. He calls attention, and with reason, to the discrepancy about his father having signalled to him before seeing him, also to his refusal to give details of his conversation with his father, and his singular account of his father's dying words. They are all, as he remarks, very much against the son.'

Holmes laughed softly to himself, and stretched himself out upon the cushioned seat. 'Both you and the coroner have been at some pains,' said he, 'to single out the very strongest points in the young man's favour. Don't you see that you alternately give him credit for having too much imagination and too little? Too little, if he could not invent a cause of quarrel which would give him the sympathy of the jury; too much, if he evolved from his own inner consciousness anything so *outré* as a dying reference to a rat, and the incident of the vanishing cloth. No, sir, I shall approach this case from the point of view that what this young man says is true, and we shall see whither that hypothesis will lead us. And now here is my pocket Petrarch, and not another word shall I say of this case until we are on the scene of action. We lunch at Swindon, and I see that we shall be there in twenty minutes.'

It was nearly four o'clock when we at last, after passing through the beautiful Stroud Valley and over the broad gleaming Severn, found ourselves at the pretty little country town of Ross. A lean, ferret-like man, furtive and sly-looking, was waiting for us upon the platform. In spite of the light brown dustcoat and leather leggings which he wore in deference to his rustic surroundings, I had no difficulty in recognizing Lestrade, of Scotland Yard. With him we drove to the 'Hereford Arms', where a room had already been engaged for us.

'I have ordered a carriage,' said Lestrade, as we sat over a cup of tea. 'I knew your energetic nature, and that you would not be happy until you had been on the scene of the crime.'

'It was very nice and complimentary of you,' Holmes answered. 'It is entirely a question of barometric pressure.'

Lestrade looked startled. 'I do not quite follow,' he said.

'How is the glass? Twenty-nine, I see. No wind, and not a cloud in the sky. I have a caseful of cigarettes here which need smoking, and the sofa is very much superior to the usual country hotel abomination. I do not think that it is probable that I shall use the carriage tonight.'

Lestrade laughed indulgently. 'You have, no doubt, already formed your conclusions from the newspapers,' he said. 'The case is as plain as a pikestaff, and the more one goes into it the plainer it becomes. Still, of course, one can't refuse a lady, and such a very positive one, too. She had heard of you, and would have your opinion, though I repeatedly told her that there was nothing which you could do which I had not already done. Why, bless my soul! here is her carriage at the door.'

He had hardly spoken before there rushed into the room one of the most lovely young women that I have ever seen in my life. Her violet eyes shining, her lips parted, a pink flush upon her cheeks, all thought of her natural reserve lost in her overpowering excitement and concern.

'Oh. Mr Sherlock Holmes!' she cried, glancing from one to the other of us, and finally, with a woman's quick intuition, fastening upon my companion, 'I am so glad that you have come. I have driven down to tell you so. I know that James didn't do it. I know it, and I want you to start upon your work knowing it, too. Never let yourself doubt upon that point. We have known each other since we were little children, and I know his faults as no one else does; but he is too tenderhearted to hurt a fly. Such a charge is absurd to anyone who really knows him.'

'I hope we may clear him, Miss Turner,' said Sherlock Holmes. 'You may rely upon my doing all that I can.'

'But you have read the evidence. You have

formed some conclusion? Do you not see some loophole, some flaw? Do you not yourself think that he is innocent?'

'I think that it is very probable.'

'There now!' she cried, throwing back her head and looking defiantly at Lestrade. 'You hear! He gives me hope.'

Lestrade shrugged his shoulders. 'I am afraid that my colleague has been a little quick in forming his conclusions,' he said.

'But he is right. Oh! I know that he is right. James never did it. And about his quarrel with his father. I am sure that the reason why he would not speak about it to the coroner was because I was concerned in it.'

'In what way?' asked Holmes.

'It is no time for me to hide anything. James and his father had many disagreements about me. Mr McCarthy was very anxious that there should be a marriage between us. James and I have always loved each other as brother and sister, but of course he is young and has seen very little of life yet, and – and – well, he naturally did not wish to do anything like that yet. So there were quarrels, and this, I am sure, was one of them.'

'And your father?' asked Holmes. 'Was he in favour of such a union?'

'No, he was averse to it also. No one but Mr McCarthy was in favour of it.' A quick blush passed over her fresh young face as Holmes shot one of his keen, questioning glances at her.

'Thank you for this information,' said he. 'May I see your father if I call tomorrow?'

'I am afraid the doctor won't allow it.'

'The doctor?'

'Yes, have you not heard? Poor father has never been strong for years back, but this has broken him down completely. He has taken to his bed, and Dr Willows says that he is a wreck, and that his nervous system is shattered. Mr McCarthy was the only man alive who had known dad in the old days in Victoria.'

'Ha! In Victoria! That is important.'

'Yes, at the mines.'

'Quite so; at the gold mines, where, as I understand, Mr Turner made his money.'

'Yes, certainly.'

'Thank you, Miss Turner. You have been of material assistance to me.'

'You will tell me if you have any news tomorrow. No doubt you will go to the prison to see James. Oh, if you do, Mr Holmes, do tell him that I know him to be innocent.'

'I will, Miss Turner.'

'I must go home now, for dad is very ill, and he misses me so if I leave him. Good-bye, and God help you in your undertaking.' She hurried from the room as impulsively as she had entered, and we heard the wheels of her carriage rattle off down the street.

'I am ashamed of you, Holmes,' said Lestrade with dignity, after a few minutes' silence. 'Why should you raise up hopes which you are bound to disappoint? I am not over-tender of heart, but I call it cruel.'

'I think that I see my way to clearing James McCarthy,' said Holmes. 'Have you an order to see him in prison?'

'Yes, but only for you and me.'

'Then I shall reconsider my resolution about going out. We have still time to take a train to Hereford and see him tonight?'

'Ample.'

'Then let us do so. Watson, I fear that you will find it very slow, but I shall only be away a couple of hours.'

I walked down to the station with them, and then wandered through the streets of the little town, finally returning to the hotel, where I lay upon the sofa and tried to interest myself in a yellow-backed novel. The puny plot of the story was so thin, however, when compared to the deep mystery through which we were groping, and I found my attention wander so constantly from the fiction to the fact, that I at last flung it across the room, and gave myself up entirely to a considera-tion of the events of the day. Supposing that this unhappy young man's story was absolutely true, then what hellish thing, what absolutely unfore-seen and extraordinary calamity, could have oc-curred between the time when he parted from his father and the moment when, drawn back by his screams, he rushed into the glade? It was something terrible and deadly. What could it be? Might not the nature of the injuries reveal something to my medical instincts? I rang the bell, and called for the weekly country paper, which contained a verbatim account of the inquest. In the surgeon's deposition it was stated that the posterior third of the left parietal bone and the left half of the occipital bone had been shattered by a heavy blow from a blunt weapon. I marked the spot upon my own head. Clearly such a blow must have been struck from behind. That was to some extent in favour of the accused, as when seen quarrelling he was face to face with his father. Still, it did not go for very much, for the older man might have turned his back before the blow fell. Still, it might be worth while to call Holmes's attention to it. Then there was the peculiar dying reference to a rat. What could that mean? It could not be delirium. A man dying from a sudden blow does not commonly become delirious. No, it was more likely to be an attempt to explain how he met his fate. But what could it indicate? I cudgelled my brains to find some possible explanation. And then the incident of the grey cloth, seen by young McCarthy. If that were true, the murderer must have dropped some part of his dress, presumably his overcoat, in his flight, and must have had the hardihood to return and carry it away at the instant when the son was kneeling with his back turned not a dozen paces off. What a tissue of mysteries and improbabilities the whole thing was!

I did not wonder at Lestrade's opinion, and yet I had so much faith in Sherlock Holmes's insight that I could not lose hope as long as every fresh fact seemed to strengthen his conviction of young McCarthy's innocence.

It was late before Sherlock Holmes returned. He came back alone, for Lestrade was staying in lodgings in the town.

'The glass still keeps very high,' he remarked, as he sat down. 'It is of importance that it should not rain before we are able to go over the ground. On the other hand, a man should be at his very best and keenest for such nice work as that, and I did not wish to do it when fagged by a long journey. I have seen young McCarthy.'

'And what did you learn from him?'

'Nothing.'

'Could he throw no light?'

'None at all. I was inclined to think at one time that he knew who had done it, and was screening him or her, but I am convinced now that he is as puzzled as everyone else. He is not a very quick-witted youth, though comely to look at, and, I should think, sound at heart.'

'I cannot admire his taste,' I remarked, 'if it is indeed a fact that he was averse to a marriage with so charming a young lady as this Miss Turner.'

'Ah, thereby hangs a rather painful tale. This fellow is madly, insanely in love with her, but some two years ago, when he was only a lad, and before he really knew her, for she had been away

five years at a boarding-school, what does the
idiot do but get into the clutches of a barmaid in
Bristol, and marry her at a registry office! No one
knows a word of the matter, but you can imagine
how maddening it must be to him to be upbraided
for not doing what he would give his very eyes to
do, but what he knows to be absolutely impossible.
It was sheer frenzy of this sort which made him
throw his hands up into the air when his father, at
their last interview, was goading him on to propose
to Miss Turner. On the other hand, he had no
means of supporting himself, and his father, who
was by all accounts a very hard man, would have
thrown him over utterly had he known the truth.
It was with his barmaid wife that he had spent the
last three days in Bristol, and his father did not
know where he was. Mark that point. It is of
importance. Good has come out of evil, however,
for the barmaid, finding from the papers that he is
in serious trouble, and likely to be hanged, has
thrown him over utterly, and has written to him
to say that she has a husband already in the
Bermuda Dockyard, so that there is really no tie
between them. I think that that bit of news has
consoled young McCarthy for all that he has
suffered.'

'But if he is innocent, who has done it?'

'Ah! who? I would call your attention very
particularly to two points. One is that the murdered man had an appointment with someone at
the Pool, and that the someone could not have

been his son, for his son was away, and he did not know when he would return. The second is that the murdered man was heard to cry "Cooee!" before he knew that his son had returned. Those are the crucial points upon which the case depends. And now let us talk about George Meredith, if you please, and we shall leave minor points until tomorrow.'

There was no rain, as Holmes had foretold, and the morning broke bright and cloudless. At nine o'clock Lestrade called for us with the carriage, and we set off for Hatherley Farm and the Boscombe Pool.

'There is serious news this morning,' Lestrade observed. 'It is said that Mr Turner, of the Hall, is so ill that his life is despaired of.'

'An elderly man, I presume?' said Holmes.

'About sixty; but his constitution has been shattered by his life abroad, and he has been in failing health for some time. This business has had a very bad effect upon him. He was an old friend of McCarthy's, and, I may add, a great benefactor to him, for I have learned that he gave him Hatherley Farm rent free.'

'Indeed! That is interesting,' said Holmes.

'Oh, yes! In a hundred other ways he has helped him. Everybody about here speaks of his kindness to him.'

'Really! Does it not strike you as a little singular that this McCarthy, who appears to have had little of his own, and to have been under such obligations to Turner, should still talk of marrying his son to Turner's daughter, who is, presumably, heiress to the estate, and that in such a very cocksure manner, as if it was merely a case of a proposal and all else would follow? It is the more strange since we know that Turner himself was averse to the idea. The daughter told us as much. Do you not deduce something from that?'

'We have got to the deductions and the inferences,' said Lestrade, winking at me. 'I find it hard enough to tackle facts, Holmes, without flying away after theories and fancies.'

'You are right,' said Holmes demurely: 'you do find it very hard to tackle the facts.'

'Anyhow, I have grasped one fact which you seem to find it difficult to get hold of,' replied Lestrade with some warmth.

'And that is?'

'That McCarthy, senior, met his death from McCarthy, junior, and that all theories to the contrary are the merest moonshine.'

'Well, moonshine is a brighter thing than fog,' said Holmes, laughing. 'But I am very much mistaken if this is not Hatherley Farm upon the left.'

'Yes, that is it.' It was a widespread, comfortable-looking building, two-storeys, slate-roofed, with great yellow blotches of lichen upon the grey walls. The drawn blinds and the smokeless chimneys, however, gave it a stricken look, as though the weight of this horror still lay heavy upon it. We called at the door, when the maid, at

Holmes's request, showed us the boots which her master wore at the time of his death, and also a pair of the son's, though not the pair which he had then had. Having measured these very carefully from seven or eight different points, Holmes desired to be led to the courtyard, from which we all followed the winding track which led to Boscombe Pool.

Sherlock Holmes was transformed when he was hot upon such a scent as this. Men who had only known the quiet thinker and logician of Baker Street would have failed to recognize him. His face flushed and darkened. His brows were drawn into two hard, black lines, while his eyes shone out from beneath them with a steely glitter. His face was bent downwards, his shoulders bowed, his lips compressed, and the veins stood out like whip-cord in his long, sinewy neck. His nostrils seemed to dilate with a purely animal lust for the chase, and his mind was so absolutely concentrated upon the matter before him, that a question or remark fell unheeded upon his ears, or at the most only provoked a quick, impatient snarl in reply. Swiftly and silently he made his way along the track which ran through the meadows, and so by way of the woods to the Boscombe Pool. It was damp, marshy ground, as is all that district, and there were marks of many feet, both upon the path and amid the short grass which bounded it on either side. Sometimes Holmes would hurry on, sometimes stop dead, and once he made quite a little *détour* into the meadow. Lestrade and I walked behind him, the detective indifferent and contemptuous, while I watched my friend with the interest which sprang from the conviction that every one of his actions was directed towards a definite end.

The Boscombe Pool, which is a reed-girt sheet of water some fifty yards across, is situated at the boundary between the Hatherley Farm and the private park of the wealthy Mr Turner. Above the woods which lined it upon the farther side we could see the red jutting pinnacles which marked the site of the rich landowner's dwelling. On the Hatherley side of the Pool, the woods grew very thick, and there was a narrow belt of sodden grass twenty paces across between the edge of the trees and the reeds which lined the lake. Lestrade showed us the exact spot at which the body had been found, and indeed, so moist was the ground, that I could plainly see the traces which had been left by the fall of the stricken man. To Holmes, as I could see by his eager face and peering eyes, very many other things were to be read upon the trampled grass. He ran round, like a dog who is picking up a scent, and then turned upon my companion.

'What did you go into the Pool for?' he asked.

'I fished about with a rake. I thought there might be some weapon or other trace. But how on earth –?'

'Oh, tut, tut! I have no time. That left foot of

yours with its inward twist is all over the place. A mole could trace it, and here it vanishes among the reeds. Oh, how simple it would all have been had I been here before they came like a herd of buffalo, and wallowed all over it. Here is where the party with the lodge-keeper came, and they have covered all tracks for six or eight feet round the body. But here are three separate tracks of the same feet.' He drew out a lens, and lay down upon his waterproof to have a better view, talking all the time rather to himself than to us. 'These are young McCarthy's feet. Twice he was walking, and once he ran swiftly so that the soles are deeply marked, and the heels hardly visible. That bears out his story. He ran when he saw his father on the ground. Then here are the father's feet as he paced up and down. What is this, then? It is the butt-end of the gun as the son stood listening. And this? Ha, ha! What have we here? Tip-toes, tip-toes! Square, too, quite unusual boots! They come, they go, they come again – of course that was for the cloak. Now where did they come from?' He ran up and down, sometimes losing, sometimes finding the track, until we were well within the edge of the wood and under the shadow of a great beech, the largest tree in the neighbour-hood. Holmes traced his way to the farther side of this, and lay down once more upon his face with a little cry of satisfaction. For a long time he re-mained there, turning over the leaves and dried sticks, gathering up what seemed to me to be dust into an envelope, and examining with his lens not only the ground, but even the bark of the tree as far as he could reach. A jagged stone was lying among the moss, and this also he carefully examined and retained. Then he followed a pathway through the wood until he came to the high-road, where all traces were lost.

'It has been a case of considerable interest,' he remarked, returning to his natural manner. 'I fancy that this grey house on the right must be the lodge. I think that I will go in and have a word with Moran, and perhaps write a little note. Having done that, we may drive back to our luncheon. You may walk to the cab, and I shall be with you presently.'

It was about ten minutes before we regained our cab, and drove back into Ross, Holmes still carrying with him the stone which he had picked up in the wood.

'This may interest you, Lestrade,' he remarked, holding it out. 'The murder was done with it.'

'I see no marks.'

'There are none.'

'How do you know, then?'

'The grass was growing under it. It had only lain there a few days. There was no sign of a place whence it had been taken. It corresponds with the injuries. There is no sign of any other weapon.'

'And the murderer?'

'Is a tall man, left-handed, limps with the right leg, wears thick-soled shooting-boots and a grey cloak, smokes Indian cigars, uses a cigar-holder, and carries a blunt penknife in his pocket. There are several other indications, but these may be enough to aid us in our search.'

Lestrade laughed. 'I am afraid that I am still a sceptic,' he said. 'Theories are all very well, but we have to deal with a hard-headed British jury.'

'*Nous verrons*,' answered Holmes calmly. 'You work your own method, and I shall work mine. I shall be busy this afternoon, and shall probably return to London by the evening train.'

'And leave your case unfinished?'

'No, finished.'

'But the mystery?'

'It is solved.'

'Who was the criminal, then?'

'The gentleman I describe.'

'But who is he?'

'Surely it would not be difficult to find out. This is not such a populous neighbourhood.'

Lestrade shrugged his shoulders. 'I am a practical man,' he said, 'and I really cannot undertake to go about the country looking for a left-handed gentleman with a game leg. I should become the laughing-stock of Scotland Yard.'

'All right,' said Holmes quietly. 'I have given you the chance. Here are your lodgings. Good-bye. I shall drop you a line before I leave.'

Having left Lestrade at his rooms we drove to our hotel, where we found lunch upon the table. Holmes was silent and buried in thought, with a pained expression upon his face, as one who finds himself in a perplexing position.

'Look here, Watson,' he said, when the cloth was cleared; 'just sit down in this chair and let me preach to you for a little. I don't quite know what to do, and I should value your advice. Light a cigar, and let me expound.'

'Pray do so.'

'Well, now, in considering this case there are two points about young McCarthy's narrative which struck us both instantly, although they impressed me in his favour and you against him. One was the fact that his father should, according to his account, cry "Cooee!" before seeing him. The other was his singular dying reference to a rat. He mumbled several words, you understand, but that was all that caught the son's ear. Now from this double point our research must commence, and we will begin it by presuming that what the lad says is absolutely true.'

'What of this "Cooee!" then?'

'Well, obviously it could not have been meant for the son. The son, as far as he knew, was in Bristol. It was mere chance that he was within earshot. The "Cooee!" was meant to attract the attention of whoever it was that he had the appointment with. But "Cooee" is a distinctly Australian cry, and one which is used between Australians. There is a strong presumption that the person whom McCarthy expected to meet at Boscombe Pool was someone who had been in Australia.'

'What of the rat, then?'

Sherlock Holmes took a folded paper from his pocket and flattened it out on the table. 'This is a map of the Colony of Victoria,' he said. 'I wired to Bristol for it last night.' He put his hand over part of the map. 'What do you read?' he asked.

'ARAT,' I read.

'And now?' He raised his hand.

'BALLARAT.'

'Quite so. That was the word the man uttered, and of which his son only caught the last two syllables. He was trying to utter the name of his murderer. So-and-so of Ballarat.'

'It is wonderful!' I exclaimed.

'It is obvious. And now, you see, I had narrowed the field down considerably. The possession of a grey garment was a third point which, granting the son's statement to be correct, was a certainty. We have come now out of mere vagueness to the definite conception of an Australian from Ballarat with a grey cloak.'

'Certainly.'

'And one who was at home in the district, for the Pool can only be approached by the farm or by the estate, where strangers could hardly wander.'

'Quite so.'

'Then comes our expedition of today. By an examination of the ground I gained the trifling details which I gave to that imbecile Lestrade, as to the personality of the criminal.'

'But how did you gain them?'

'You know my method. It is founded upon the observance of trifles.'

'His height I know that you might roughly judge from the length of his stride. His boots, too, might be told from their traces.'

'Yes, they were peculiar boots.'

'But his lameness?'

'The impression of his right foot was always less distinct than his left. He put less weight upon it. Why? Because he limped – he was lame.'

'But his left-handedness?'

'You were yourself struck by the nature of the injury as recorded by the surgeon at the inquest. The blow was struck from immediately behind, and yet was upon the left side. Now, how can that be unless it were by a left-handed man? He had stood behind that tree during the interview between the father and son. He had even smoked there. I found the ash of a cigar, which my special knowledge of tobacco ashes enabled me to pronounce as an Indian cigar. I have, as you know, devoted some attention to this, and written a little monograph on the ashes of 140 different varieties of pipe, cigar, and cigarette tobacco. Having found the ash, I then looked round and discovered the stump among the moss where he had tossed it. It was an Indian cigar, of the variety which are rolled in Rotterdam.'

'And the cigar-holder?'

'I could see that the end had not been in his

mouth. Therefore he used a holder. The tip had been cut off, not bitten off, but the cut was not a clean one, so I deduced a blunt penknife.'

'Holmes,' I said, 'you have drawn a net round this man from which he cannot escape, and you have saved an innocent human life as truly as if you had cut the cord which was hanging him. I see the direction in which all this points. The culprit is –'

'Mr John Turner,' cried the hotel waiter, opening the door of our sitting-room, and ushering in a visitor.

The man who entered was a strange and impressive figure. His slow, limping step and bowed shoulders gave the appearance of decrepitude, and yet his hard, deep-lined, craggy features, and his enormous limbs showed that he was possessed of unusual strength of body and of character. His tangled beard, grizzled hair, and outstanding, drooping eyebrows combined to give an air of dignity and power to his appearance, but his face was of an ashen white, while his lips and the corners of his nostrils were tinged with a shade of blue. It was clear to me at a glance that he was in the grip of some deadly and chronic disease.

'Pray sit down on the sofa,' said Holmes gently. 'You had my note?'

'Yes, the lodge-keeper brought it up. You said that you wished to see me here to avoid scandal.'

'I thought people would talk if I went to the Hall.'

'And why did you wish to see me?' He looked across at my companion with despair in his weary eyes, as though his question were already answered.

'Yes,' said Holmes, answering the look rather than the words. 'It is so. I know all about McCarthy.'

The old man sank his face in his hands. 'God help me!' he cried. 'But I would not have let the young man come to harm. I give you my word that I would have spoken out if it went against him at the Assizes.'

'I am glad to hear you say so,' said Holmes gravely.

'I would have spoken now had it not been for my dear girl. It would break her heart – it will break her heart when she hears that I am arrested.'

'It may not come to that,' said Holmes.

'What!'

'I am no official agent. I understand that it was your daughter who required my presence here, and I am acting in her interests. Young McCarthy must be got off, however.'

'I am a dying man,' said old Turner. 'I have had diabetes for years. My doctor says it is a question whether I shall live a month. Yet I would rather die under my own roof than in gaol.'

Holmes rose and sat down, at the table with his pen in his hand and a bundle of paper before him. 'Just tell us the truth,' he said. 'I shall jot down the

facts. You will sign it, and Watson here can witness it. Then I could produce your confession at
the last extremity to save young McCarthy. I
promise you that I shall not use it unless it is
absolutely needed.'

'It's as well,' said the old man; 'it's a question
whether I shall live to the Assizes, so it matters
little to me, but I should wish to spare Alice the
shock. And now I will make the thing clear to
you; it has been a long time in the acting, but will
not take me long to tell.

'You didn't know this dead man, McCarthy.
He was a devil incarnate. I tell you that. God keep
you out of the clutches of such a man as he. His
grip has been upon me these twenty years, and he
has blasted my life. I'll tell you first how I came
to be in his power.

'It was in the early 'sixties at the diggings. I
was a young chap then, hot-blooded and reckless,
ready to turn my hand to anything; I got among
bad companions, took to drink, had no luck with
my claim, took to the bush, and, in a word became
what you would call over here a highway robber.
There were six of us, and we had a wild, free life
of it, sticking up a station from time to time, or
stopping the wagons on the road to the diggings.
Black Jack of Ballarat was the name I went under,
and our party is still remembered in the colony as
the Ballarat Gang.

'One day a gold convoy came down from Ballarat to Melbourne, and we lay in wait for it and

attacked it. There were six troopers and six of us, so it was a close thing, but we emptied four of their saddles at the first volley. Three of our boys were killed, however, before we got the swag. I put my pistol to the head of the wagon-driver, who was this very man McCarthy. I wish to the Lord that I had shot him then, but I spared him though I saw his wicked little eyes fixed on my face, as though to remember every feature. We got away with the gold, became wealthy men, and made our way over to England without being suspected. There I parted from my old pals, and determined to settle down to a quiet and respectable life. I bought this estate which chanced to be in the market, and I set myself to do a little good with my money, to make up for the way in which I had earned it. I married, too, and though my wife died young, she left me my dear little Alice. Even when she was just a baby her wee hand seemed to lead me down the right path as nothing else had ever done. In a word, I turned over a new leaf, and did my best to make up for the past. All was going well when McCarthy laid his grip upon me.

'I had gone up to town about an investment, and I met him in Regent Street with hardly a coat to his back, or a boot to his foot.

'"Here we are, Jack," says he, touching me on the arm; "we'll be as good as a family to you. There's two of us, me and my son, and you can have the keeping of us. If you don't – it's a fine, law-abiding country is England, and there's always a policeman within hail."

'Well, down they came to the West Country, there was no shaking them off, and there they have lived rent free on my best land ever since. There was no rest for me, no peace, no forgetfulness; turn where I would, there was his cunning, grinning face at my elbow. It grew worse as Alice grew up, for he soon saw I was more afraid of her knowing my past than of the police. Whatever he wanted he must have, and whatever it was I gave him without question, land, money, houses, until at last he asked for a thing which I could not give. He asked for Alice.

'His son, you see, had grown up, and so had my girl, and as I was known to be in weak health, it seemed a fine stroke to him that his lad should step into the whole property. But there I was firm. I would not have his cursed stock mixed with mine; not that I had any dislike to the lad, but his blood was in him, and that was enough. I stood firm. McCarthy threatened. I braved him to do his worst. We were to meet at the Pool midway between our houses to talk it over.

'When I went down there I found him talking with his son, so I smoked a cigar, and waited behind a tree until he should be alone. But as I listened to his talk all that was black and bitter in me seemed to come uppermost. He was urging his son to marry my daughter with as little regard for what she might think as if she were a slut from off the streets. It drove me mad to think that I and all that I held most dear should be in the power of such a man as this. Could I not snap the bond? I was already a dying and a desperate man. Though clear of mind and fairly strong of limb, I knew that my own fate was sealed. But my memory and my girl! Both could be saved, if I could but silence that foul tongue. I did it, Mr Holmes. I would do it again. Deeply as I have sinned, I have led a life of martyrdom to atone for it. But that my girl should be entangled in the same meshes which held me was more than I could suffer. I struck him down with no more compunction than if he had been some foul and venomous beast. His cry brought back his son; but I had gained the cover of the wood, though I was forced to go back to fetch the cloak which I had dropped in my flight. That is the true story, gentlemen, of all that occurred.'

'Well, it is not for me to judge you,' said Holmes, as the old man signed the statement which had been drawn out. 'I pray that we may never be exposed to such a temptation.'

'I pray not, sir. And what do you intend to do?'

'In view of your health, nothing. You are yourself aware that you will soon have to answer for your deed at a higher court than the Assizes. I will keep your confession, and, if McCarthy is condemned, I shall be forced to use it. If not, it shall never be seen by mortal eye; and your secret, whether you be alive or dead, shall be safe with us.'

'Farewell! then,' said the old man solemnly. 'Your own death-beds, when they come, will be the easier for the thought of the peace which you have given to mine.' Tottering and shaking in all his giant frame, he stumbled slowly from the room.

'God help us!' said Holmes, after a long silence. 'Why does Fate play such tricks with poor helpless worms? I never hear of such a case as this that I do not think of Baxter's words, and say: "There, but for the grace of God, goes Sherlock Holmes."'

James McCarthy was acquitted at the Assizes, on the strength of a number of objections which had been drawn out by Holmes, and submitted to the defending counsel. Old Turner lived for seven months after our interview, but he is now dead; and there is every prospect that the son and daughter may come to live happily together, in ignorance of the black cloud which rests upon their past.

THE THREE STUDENTS

It was in the year '95 that a combination of events, into which I need not enter, caused Mr Sherlock Holmes and myself to spend some weeks in one of our great University towns, and it was during this time that the small but instructive adventure which I am about to relate befell us. It will be obvious that any details which would help the reader to exactly identify the college or the criminal would be injudicious and offensive. So painful a scandal may well be allowed to die out. With due discretion the incident itself may, however, be described, since it serves to illustrate some of those qualities for which my friend was remarkable. I will endeavour in my statement to avoid such terms as would serve to limit the events to any particular place, or give a clue as to the people concerned.

We were residing at the time in furnished lodgings close to a library where Sherlock Holmes was pursuing some laborious researches in Early English charters – researches which led to results so striking that they may be the subject of one of my future narratives. Here it was that one evening we received a visit from an acquaintance, Mr Hilton Soames, tutor and lecturer at the College of St Luke's. Mr Soames was a tall, spare man, of a nervous and excitable temperament. I had always known him to be restless in his manner, but on this particular occasion he was in such a state of uncontrollable agitation that it was clear something very unusual had occurred.

'I trust, Mr Holmes, that you can spare me a few hours of your valuable time. We have had a very painful incident at St Luke's, and really, but for the happy chance of your being in the town, I should have been at a loss what to do.'

'I am very busy now, and I desire no distractions,' my friend answered. 'I should much prefer that you called in the aid of the police.'

'No, no, my dear sir; such a course is utterly impossible. When once the law is evoked it cannot be stayed again, and this is just one of those cases where, for the credit of the college, it is most essential to avoid scandal. Your discretion is as well known as your powers, and you are the one man in the world who can help me. I beg you, Mr Holmes, to do what you can.'

My friend's temper had not improved since he had been deprived of the congenial surroundings of Baker Street. Without his scrap-books, his chemicals, and his homely untidiness, he was an uncomfortable man. He shrugged his shoulders in ungracious acquiescence, while our visitor in hurried words and with much excitable gesticulation poured forth his story.

'I must explain to you, Mr Holmes, that tomorrow is the first day of the examination for the Fortescue Scholarship. I am one of the examiners. My subject is Greek, and the first of the papers consists of a large passage of Greek translation which the candidate has not seen. This passage is printed on the examination paper, and it would naturally be an immense advantage if the candidate could prepare it in advance. For this reason great care is taken to keep the paper secret.

'Today about three o'clock the proofs of this paper arrived from the printers. The exercise consists of half a chapter of Thucydides. I had to read it over carefully, as the text must be absolutely correct. At four-thirty my task was not yet completed. I had, however, promised to take tea in a friend's rooms, so I left the proof upon my desk. I was absent rather more than an hour. You are aware, Mr Holmes, that our college doors are double – a green baize one within and a heavy oak one without. As I approached my outer door I was amazed to see a key in it. For an instant I imagined that I had left my own there, but on feeling in my pocket I found that it was all right. The only duplicate which existed, so far as I knew, was that which belonged to my servant, Bannister, a man who has looked after my room for ten years, and whose honesty is absolutely above suspicion. I found that the key was indeed his, that he had entered my room to know if I wanted tea, and that he had very carelessly left the key in the door when he came out. His visit to my room must have been within a very few minutes of my leaving it. His forgetfulness about the key would have mattered little upon any other occasion, but on this one day it has produced the most deplorable consequences.

'The moment I looked at my table I was aware that someone had rummaged among my papers. The proof was in three long slips. I had left them all together. Now I found that one of them was lying on the floor, one was on the side-table near the window, and the third was where I had left it.'

Holmes stirred for the first time.

'The first page on the floor, the second in the window, and the third where you left it,' said he.

'Exactly, Mr Holmes. You amaze me. How could you possibly know that?'

'Pray continue your very interesting statement.'

'For an instant I imagined that Bannister had taken the unpardonable liberty of examining my papers. He denied it, however, with the utmost earnestness, and I am convinced that he was speaking the truth. The alternative was that someone passing had observed the key in the door, had known that I was out, and had entered to look at the papers. A large sum of money is at stake, for the scholarship is a very valuable one, and an unscrupulous man might very well run a risk in order to gain advantage over his fellows.

'Bannister was very much upset by the incident. He had nearly fainted when we found that the papers had undoubtedly been tampered with. I gave him a little brandy and left him collapsed in a chair while I made a most careful examination of the room. I soon saw that the intruder had left other traces of his presence besides the rumpled papers. On the table in the window were several shreds from a pencil which had been sharpened. A broken tip of lead was lying there also. Evidently the rascal had copied the paper in a great hurry, had broken his pencil, and had been compelled to put a fresh point to it.'

'Excellent!' said Holmes, who was recovering his good humour as his attention became more engrossed by the case. 'Fortune has been your friend.'

'This was not all. I have a new writing-table with a fine surface of red leather. I am prepared to swear, and so is Bannister, that it was smooth and unstained. Now I found a clean cut in it about three inches long – not a mere scratch, but a positive cut. Not only this, but on the table I found a small ball of black dough, or clay, with specks of something which looks like sawdust in it. I am convinced that these marks were left by the man who rifled the papers. There were no footmarks and no other evidence as to his identity. I was at my wits' end, when suddenly the happy thought occurred to me that you were in the town, and I came straight round to put the matter into your hands. Do help me, Mr Holmes! You see my dilemma. Either I must find the man, or else the examination must be postponed until fresh papers are prepared, and since this cannot be done without explanation, there will ensue a hideous scandal, which will throw a cloud not only on the college but on the University. Above all things, I desire to settle the matter quietly and discreetly.'

'I shall be happy to look into it and to give you such advice as I can,' said Holmes, rising and putting on his overcoat. 'This case is not entirely devoid of interest. Has anyone visited you in your room after the papers came to you?'

'Yes, young Daulat Ras, an Indian student who lives on the same stair, came in to ask me some particulars about the examination.'

'For which he was entered?'

'Yes.'

'And the papers were on your table?'

'To the best of my belief they were rolled up.'

'But might be recognized as proofs?'

'Possibly.'

'No one else in your room?'

'No.'

'Did anyone know that these proofs would be there?'

'No one save the printer.'

'Did this man Bannister know?'

'No, certainly not. No one knew.'

'Where is Bannister now?'

'He was very ill, poor fellow! I left him collapsed in the chair. I was in such a hurry to come to you.'

'You left your door open?'

'I locked the papers up first.'

'Then it amounts to this, Mr Soames, that unless the Indian student recognized the roll as being proofs, the man who tampered with them came upon them accidentally without knowing that they were there.'

'So it seems to me.'

Holmes gave an enigmatic smile.

'Well,' said he, 'let us go round. Not one of your cases, Watson – mental, not physical. All right; come if you want to. Now, Mr Soames – at your disposal!'

The sitting-room of our client opened by a long, low, latticed window on to the ancient lichen-tinted court of the old college. A Gothic arched door led to a worn stone staircase. On the ground floor was the tutor's room. Above were three students, one on each storey. It was already twilight when we reached the scene of our problem. Holmes halted and looked earnestly at the window. Then he approached it, and, standing on tiptoe, with his neck craned, he looked into the room.

'He must have entered through the door. There is no opening except the one pane,' said our learned guide.

'Dear me!' said Holmes, and he smiled in a

singular way as he glanced at our companion. 'Well, if there is nothing to be learned here we had best go inside.'

The lecturer unlocked the outer door and ushered us into his room. We stood at the entrance while Holmes made an examination of the carpet.

'I am afraid there are no signs here,' said he. 'One could hardly hope for any upon so dry a day. Your servant seems to have quite recovered. You left him in a chair, you say; which chair?'

'By the window there.'

'I see. Near this little table. You can come in now. I have finished with the carpet. Let us take the little table first. Of course, what has happened is very clear. The man entered and took the papers, sheet by sheet, from the central table. He carried them over to the window table, because from there he could see if you came across the courtyard, and so could effect an escape.'

'As a matter of fact, he could not,' said Soames, 'for I entered by the side-door.'

'Ah, that's good! Well, anyhow, that was in his mind. Let me see the three strips. No finger impressions – no! Well, he carried over this one first and he copied it. How long would it take him to do that, using every possible contraction? A quarter of an hour, not less. Then he tossed it down and seized the next. He was in the midst of that when your return caused him to make a very hurried retreat – *very* hurried, since he had not time to replace the papers which would tell you that he had been there. You were not aware of any hurrying feet on the stair as you entered the outer door?'

'No, I can't say I was.'

'Well, he wrote so furiously that he broke his pencil, and had, as you observe, to sharpen it again. This is of interest, Watson. The pencil was not an ordinary one. It was above the usual size with a soft lead; the outer colour was dark blue, the maker's name was printed in silver lettering, and the piece remaining is only about an inch and a half long. Look for such a pencil, Mr Soames, and you have got your man. When I add that he possesses a large and very blunt knife, you have an additional aid.'

Mr Soames was somewhat overwhelmed by this flood of information. 'I can follow the other points,' said he, 'but really in this matter of the length –'

Holmes held out a small chip with the letters NN and a space of clear wood after them.

'You see?'

'No, I fear that even now –'

'Watson, I have always done you an injustice. There are others. What could this NN be? It is at the end of a word. You are aware that Johann Faber is the most common maker's name. Is it not clear that there is just as much of the pencil left as usually follows the Johann?' He held the small table side-ways to the electric light. 'I was hoping that if the paper on which he wrote was thin some trace of it might come through upon this polished surface. No, I see nothing. I don't think there is anything more to be learned here. Now for the central table. This small pellet is, I presume, the black doughy mass you spoke of. Roughly pyramidal in shape and hollowed out, I perceive. As you say, there appear to be grains of sawdust in it. Dear me, this is very interesting. And the cut, a positive tear, I see. It began with a thin scratch and ended in a jagged hole. I am much indebted to you for directing my attention to this case, Mr Soames. Where does that door lead to?'

'To my bedroom.'

'Have you been in it since your adventure?'

'No; I came straight away for you.'

'I should like to have a glance round. What a charming, old-fashioned room! Perhaps you will kindly wait a minute until I have examined the floor. No, I see nothing. What about this curtain? You hang your clothes behind it. If anyone were forced to conceal himself in this room he must do it there, since the bed is too low and the wardrobe too shallow. No one there, I suppose?'

As Holmes drew the curtain I was aware, from some little rigidity and alertness of his attitude, that he was prepared for an emergency. As a matter of fact the drawn curtain disclosed nothing but three or four suits of clothes hanging from a line of pegs. Holmes turned away, and stooped suddenly to the floor.

'Halloa! What's this?' said he.

It was a small pyramid of black, putty-like stuff, exactly like the one upon the table of the study. Holmes held it out on his open palm in the glare of the electric light.

'Your visitor seems to have left traces in your bedroom as well as in your sitting-room, Mr Soames.'

'What could he have wanted there?'

'I think it is clear enough. You came back by an unexpected way, and so he had no warning until you were at the very door. What could he do? He caught up everything which would betray him, and he rushed into your bedroom to conceal himself.'

'Good gracious, Mr Holmes, do you mean to tell me that all the time I was talking to Bannister in this room we had the man prisoner if we had only known it?'

'So I read it.'

'Surely there is another alternative, Mr Holmes? I don't know whether you observed my bedroom window.'

'Lattice-paned, lead framework, three separate windows, one swinging on a hinge and large enough to admit a man.'

'Exactly. And it looks out on an angle of the court-yard so as to be partly invisible. The man might have effected his entrance there, left traces as he passed through the bedroom, and, finally, finding the door open, have escaped that way.'

Holmes shook his head impatiently.

'Let us be practical,' said he. 'I understand you to say that there are three students who use this stair and are in the habit of passing your door?'

'Yes, there are.'

'And they are all in this examination?'

'Yes.'

'Have you any reason to suspect any one of them more than the others?'

Soames hesitated.

'It is a very delicate question,' said he. 'One hardly likes to throw suspicion where there are no proofs.'

'Let us hear the suspicions. I will look after the proofs.'

'I will tell you, then, in a few words, the character of the three men who inhabit these rooms. The lower of the three is Gilchrist, a fine scholar and athlete; plays in the Rugby team and the cricket team for the college, and got his Blue for the hurdles and the long jump. He is a fine, manly fellow. His father was the notorious Sir Jabez Gilchrist, who ruined himself on the Turf. My scholar has been left very poor, but he is hard-working and industrious. He will do well.

'The second floor is inhabited by Daulat Ras, the Indian. He is a quiet, inscrutable fellow, as most of those Indians are. He is well up in his work, though his Greek is his weak subject. He is steady and methodical.

'The top floor belongs to Miles McLaren. He is a brilliant fellow when he chooses to work – one of the brightest intellects of the University; but he is wayward, dissipated, and unprincipled. He was nearly expelled over a card scandal in his first year. He has been idling all this term, and he must look forward with dread to the examination.'

'Then it is he whom you suspect?'

'I dare not go so far as that. But of the three he is perhaps the least unlikely.'

'Exactly. Now, Mr Soames, let us have a look at your servant, Bannister.'

He was a little, white-faced, clean-shaven, grizzly-haired fellow of fifty. He was still suffering from this sudden disturbance of the quiet routine of his life. His plump face was twitching with his nervousness, and his fingers could not keep still.

'We are investigating this unhappy business, Bannister,' said his master.

'Yes, sir.'

'I understand,' said Holmes, 'that you left your key in the door.'

'Yes, sir.'

'Was it not very extraordinary that you should do this on the very day when there were these papers inside?'

'It was most unfortunate, sir. But I have occasionally done the same thing at other times.'

'When did you enter the room?'

'It was about half-past four. That is Mr Soames's tea-time.'

'How long did you stay?'

'When I saw that he was absent I withdrew at once.'

'Did you look at these papers on the table?'

'No, sir; certainly not.'

'How came you to leave the key in the door?'

'I had the tea-tray in my hand. I thought I would come back for the key. Then I forgot.'

'Has the outer door a spring lock?'

'No, sir.'

'Then it was open all the time?'

'Yes, sir.'

'Anyone in the room could get out?'

'Yes, sir.'

'When Mr Soames returned and called for you, you were very much disturbed?'

'Yes, sir. Such a thing has never happened during the many years that I have been here. I nearly fainted, sir.'

'So I understand. Where were you when you began to feel bad?'

'Where was I, sir? Why, here, near the door.'

'That is singular, because you sat down in that chair over yonder near the corner. Why did you pass these other chairs?'

'I don't know, sir. It didn't matter to me where I sat.'

'I really don't think he knew much about it, Mr Holmes. He was looking very bad – quite ghastly.'

'You stayed here when your master left?'

'Only for a minute or so. Then I locked the door and went to my room.'

'Whom do you suspect?'

'Oh, I would not venture to say, sir. I don't believe there is any gentleman in this University who is capable of profiting by such an action. No, sir, I'll not believe it.'

'Thank you; that will do,' said Holmes. 'Oh, one more word. You have not mentioned to any of the three gentlemen whom you attend that anything is amiss?'

'No, sir; not a word.'

'You haven't seen any of them?'

'No, sir.'

'Very good. Now, Mr Soames, we will take a walk in the quadrangle, if you please.'

Three yellow squares of light shone above us in the gathering gloom.

'Your three birds are all in their nests,' said Holmes, looking up. 'Halloa! What's that? One of them seems restless enough.'

It was the Indian, whose dark silhouette appeared suddenly upon the blind. He was pacing swiftly up and down his room.

'I should like to have a peep at each of them,' said Holmes. 'Is it possible?'

'No difficulty in the world,' Soames answered. 'This set of rooms is quite the oldest in the college, and it is not unusual for visitors to go over them. Come along, and I will personally conduct you.'

'No names, please!' said Holmes, as we knocked at Gilchrist's door. A tall, flaxen-haired, slim young fellow opened it, and made us welcome when he understood our errand. There were some really curious pieces of medieval domestic architecture within. Holmes was so charmed with one of them that he insisted on drawing it on his notebook, broke his pencil, had to borrow one from our host, and finally borrowed a knife to sharpen his own. The same curious accident happened to him in the rooms of the Indian – a silent little hook-nosed fellow, who eyed us askance and was obviously glad when Holmes's architectural studies had come to an end. I could not see that in either case Holmes had come upon the clue for which he was searching. Only at the third did our visit prove abortive. The outer door would not open to our knock, and nothing more substantial than a torrent of bad language came from behind it. 'I don't care who you are. You can go to blazes!' roared the angry voice. 'Tomorrow's the exam, and I won't be drawn by anyone.'

'A rude fellow,' said our guide, flushing with anger as we withdrew down the stair. 'Of course, he did not realize that it was I who was knocking, but none the less his conduct was very uncourteous, and, indeed, under the circumstances, rather suspicious.'

Holmes's response was a curious one.

'Can you tell me his exact height?' he asked.

'Really, Mr Holmes, I cannot undertake to say. He is taller than the Indian, not so tall as Gilchrist. I suppose five foot six would be about it.'

'That is very important,' said Holmes. 'And now, Mr Soames, I wish you good night.'

Our guide cried aloud in his astonishment and dismay. 'Good gracious, Mr Holmes, you are surely not going to leave me in this abrupt fashion! You don't seem to realize the position. Tomorrow is the examination. I must take some definite action tonight. I cannot allow the examination to be held if one of the papers has been tampered with. The situation must be faced.'

'You must leave it as it is. I shall drop round early tomorrow morning and chat the matter over. It is possible that I may be in a position then to indicate some course of action. Meanwhile you change nothing – nothing at all.'

'Very good, Mr Holmes.'

'You can be perfectly easy in your mind. We shall certainly find some way out of your difficulties. I will take the black clay with me, also the pencil cuttings. Goodbye.'

When we were out in the darkness of the quadrangle we again looked up at the windows. The Indian still paced his room. The others were invisible.

'Well, Watson, what do you think of it?' Holmes asked as we came out into the main street. 'Quite a little parlour game – sort of three-card trick, is it not? There are your three men. It must be one of them. You take your choice. Which is yours?'

'The foul-mouthed fellow at the top. He is the one with the worst record. And yet that Indian was a sly fellow also. Why should he be pacing his room all the time?'

'There is nothing in that. Many men do it when they are trying to learn anything by heart.'

'He looked at us in a queer way.'

'So would you if a flock of strangers came in on you when you were preparing for an examination next day, and every moment was of value. No, I see nothing in that. Pencils, too, and knives – all was satisfactory. But that fellow *does* puzzle me.'

'Who?'

'Why, Bannister, the servant. What's his game in the matter?'

'He impressed me as being a perfectly honest man.'

'So he did me. That's the puzzling part. Why should a perfectly honest man – well, well, here's a large stationer's. We shall begin our researches here.'

There were only four stationers of any consequence in the town, and at each Holmes produced his pencil chips and bid high for a duplicate. All were agreed that one could be ordered, but that it was not a usual size of pencil, and that it was seldom kept in stock. My friend did not appear to be depressed by his failure, but shrugged his shoulders in half-humorous resignation.

'No good, my dear Watson. This, the best and only final clue, has run to nothing. But, indeed, I have little doubt that we can build up a sufficient case without it. By Jove! my dear fellow, it is nearly nine, and the landlady babbled of green peas at seven-thirty. What with your eternal tobacco, Watson, and your irregularity at meals, I expect that you will get notice to quit, and that I shall share your downfall – not, however, before we have solved the problem of the nervous tutor, the careless servant, and the three enterprising students.'

Holmes made no further allusion to the matter that day, though he sat lost in thought for a long time after our belated dinner. At eight in the morning he came into my room just as I finished my toilet.

'Well, Watson,' said he, 'it is time we went down to St Luke's. Can you do without breakfast?'

'Certainly.'

'Soames will be in a dreadful fidget until we are able to tell him something positive.'

'Have you anything positive to tell him?'

'I think so.'

'You have formed a conclusion?'

'Yes, my dear Watson; I have solved the mystery.'

'But what fresh evidence could you have got?'

'Aha! It is not for nothing that I have turned myself out of bed at the untimely hour of six. I have put in two hours' hard work and covered at least five miles, with something to show for it. Look at that!'

He held out his hand. On the palm were three little pyramids of black, doughy clay.

'Why, Holmes, you had only two yesterday!'

'And one more this morning. It is a fair argument, that wherever No. 3 came from is also the source of Nos. 1 and 2. Eh, Watson? Well, come along and put friend Soames out of his pain.'

The unfortunate tutor was certainly in a state of pitiable agitation when we found him in his chambers. In a few hours the examinations would commence and he was still in the dilemma between making the facts public and allowing the culprit to compete for the valuable scholarship. He could hardly stand still, so great was his mental agitation, and he ran towards Holmes with two eager hands outstretched.

'Thank Heaven that you have come! I feared that you had given it up in despair. What am I to do? Shall the examination proceed?'

'Yes; let it proceed by all means.'

'But this rascal –?'

'He shall not compete.'

'You know him?'

'I think so. If this matter is not to become public we must give ourselves certain powers, and resolve ourselves into a small private court martial. You there, if you please, Soames! Watson, you here! I'll take the armchair in the middle. I think that we are now sufficiently imposing to strike terror into a guilty breast. Kindly ring the bell!'

Bannister entered, and shrank back in evident surprise and fear at our judicial appearance.

'You will kindly close the door,' said Holmes. 'Now, Bannister, will you please tell us the truth about yesterday's incident?'

The man turned white to the roots of his hair.

'I have told you everything, sir.'

'Nothing to add?'

'Nothing at all, sir.'

'Well, then, I must make some suggestions to you. When you sat down on that chair yesterday, did you do so in order to conceal some object which would have shown who had been in the room?'

Bannister's face was ghastly.

'No, sir; certainly not.'

'It is only a suggestion,' said Holmes suavely. 'I frankly admit that I am unable to prove it. But it seems probable enough, since the moment that Mr Soames's back was turned you released the man who was hiding in that bedroom.'

Bannister licked his dry lips.

'There was no man, sir.'

'Ah, that's a pity, Bannister. Up to now you may have spoken the truth, but now I know that you have lied.'

The man's face set in sullen defiance.

'There was no man, sir.'

'Come, come, Bannister.'

'No, sir; there was no one.'

'In that case you can give us no further information. Would you please remain in the room? Stand over there near the bedroom door. Now, Soames, I am going to ask you to have the great kindness to go up to the room of young Gilchrist, and to ask him to step down into yours.'

An instant later the tutor returned, bringing with him the student. He was a fine figure of a man, tall, lithe, and agile, with a springy step and a pleasant, open face. His troubled blue eyes glanced at each of us, and finally rested with an expression of blank dismay upon Bannister in the farther corner.

'Just close the door,' said Holmes. 'Now, Mr Gilchrist, we are all quite alone here, and no one need ever know one word of what passes between us. We can be perfectly frank with each other. We want to know, Mr Gilchrist, how you, an honourable man, ever came to commit such an action as that of yesterday?'

The unfortunate young man staggered back, and cast a look full of horror and reproach at Bannister.

'No, no, Mr Gilchrist, sir; I never said a word – never one word!' cried the servant.

'No, but you have now,' said Holmes. 'Now, sir, you must see that after Bannister's words your position is hopeless, and that your only chance lies in a frank confession.'

For a moment Gilchrist, with upraised hand, tried to control his writhing features. The next he had thrown himself on his knees beside the table, and, burying his face in his hands, he burst into a storms of passionate sobbing.

'Come, come,' said Holmes kindly; 'it is human to err, and at least no one can accuse you of being a callous criminal. Perhaps it would be easier for you if I were to tell Mr Soames what occurred, and you can check me where I am wrong. Shall I do so? Well, well, don't trouble to answer. Listen, and see that I do you no injustice.

'From the moment, Mr Soames, that you said to me that no one, not even Bannister, could have told that the papers were in your room, the case began to take a definite shape in my mind. The printer one could, of course, dismiss. He could examine the papers in his own office. The Indian I also thought nothing of. If the proofs were in the roll he could not possibly know what they were. On the other hand, it seemed an unthinkable coincidence that a man should dare to enter the room, and that by chance on that very day the papers were on the table. I dismissed that. The man who entered knew that the papers were there. How did he know?

'When I approached your room I examined the window. You amused me by supposing that I was contemplating the possibility of someone having in broad daylight, under the eyes of all these opposite rooms, forced himself through it. Such an idea was absurd. I was measuring how tall a man would need to be in order to see as he passed what papers were on the central table. I am six feet high, and I could do it with an effort. No one less than that would have a chance. Already, you see, I had reason to think that if one of your three students was a man of unusual height he was the most worth watching of the three.

'I entered, and I took you into my confidence as to the suggestions of the side-table. Of the centre table I could make nothing, until in your description of Gilchrist you mentioned that he was a long-distance jumper. Then the whole thing came to me in an instant, and I only needed certain corroborative proofs, which I speedily obtained.

'What happened was this. This young fellow had employed his afternoon at the athletic grounds, where he had been practising the jump. He returned carrying his jumping-shoes, which are provided, as you are aware, with several spikes. As he passed your window he saw, by means of his great height, these proofs upon your table, and conjectured what they were. No harm would have been done had it not been that as he passed your door he perceived the key which had been left by the carelessness of your servant. A sudden impulse came over him to enter and see if they were indeed the proofs. It was not a dangerous exploit, for he could always pretend that he had simply looked in to ask a question.

'Well, when he saw that they were indeed the proofs, it was then that he yielded to temptation.

He put his shoes on the table. What was it you put on that chair near the window?'

'Gloves,' said the young man.

Holmes looked triumphantly at Bannister.

'He put his gloves on the chair, and he took the proofs, sheet by sheet, to copy them. He thought the tutor must return by the main gate, and that he would see him. As we know, he came back by the side-gate. Suddenly he heard him at the very door. There was no possible escape. He forgot his gloves, but he caught up his shoes and darted into the bedroom. You observe that the scratch on that table is slight at one side, but deepens in the direction of the bedroom door. That in itself is enough to show us that the shoes had been drawn in that direction, and that the culprit had taken refuge there. The earth round the spike had been left on the table, and a second sample was loosened and fell in the bedroom. I may add that I walked out to the athletic grounds this morning, saw that tenacious black clay is used in the jumping-pit, and carried away a specimen of it, together with some of the fine tan or sawdust which is strewn over it to prevent the athlete from slipping. Have I told the truth, Mr Gilchrist?'

The student had drawn himself erect.

'Yes, sir, it is true,' said he.

'Good heavens, have you nothing to add?' cried Soames.

'Yes, sir, I have, but the shock of this disgrace-ful exposure has bewildered me. I have a letter here, Mr Soames, which I wrote to you early this morning in the middle of a restless night. It was before I knew that my sin had found me out. Here it is, sir. You will see that I have said, "I have determined not to go in for the examination. I have been offered a commission in the Rhodesian Police, and I am going out to South Africa at once."'

'I am indeed pleased to hear that you did not intend to profit by your unfair advantage,' said Soames. 'But why did you change your purpose?'

Gilchrist pointed to Bannister.

'There is the man who sent me in the right path,' said he.

'Come now, Bannister,' said Holmes. 'It will be clear to you from what I have said that only you could have let this young man out, since you were left in the room and must have locked the door when you went out. As to his escaping by that window, it was incredible. Can you not clear up the last point in this mystery, and tell us the reason for your action?'

'It was simple enough, sir, if you had only known; but with all your cleverness it was impossible that you could know. Time was, sir, when I was butler to old Sir Jabez Gilchrist, this young gentleman's father. When he was ruined I came to the college as servant, but I never forgot my old employer because he was down in the world. I watched his son all I could for the sake of the old days. Well, sir, when I came into this room yesterday when the alarm was given, the first thing I saw was Mr Gilchrist's tan gloves a-lying in that chair. I knew those gloves well, and I understood their message. If Mr Soames saw them the game was up. I flopped down into that chair, and nothing would budge me until Mr Soames went for you. Then out came my poor young master, whom I had dandled on my knee, and confessed it all to me. Wasn't it natural, sir, that I should save him, and wasn't it natural also that I should try to speak to him as his dead father would have done, and make him understand that he could not profit by such a deed? Could you blame me, sir?'

'No, indeed!' said Holmes heartily, springing to his feet. 'Well, Soames, I think we have cleared your little problem up, and our breakfast awaits us at home. Come, Watson! As to you, sir, I trust that a bright future awaits you in Rhodesia. For once you have fallen low. Let us see in the future how high you can rise.'

The Noble Bachelor

The Lord St Simon marriage, and its curious termination, have long since ceased to be a subject of interest in those exalted circles in which the unfortunate bridegroom moves. Fresh scandals have eclipsed it, and their more piquant details have drawn the gossips away from this four-year-old drama. As I have reason to believe, however, that the full facts have never been revealed to the general public, and as my friend Sherlock Holmes had a considerable share in clearing the matter up, I feel that no memoir of him would be complete without some little sketch of this remarkable episode.

It was a few weeks before my own marriage, during the days when I was still sharing rooms with Holmes in Baker Street, that he came home from an afternoon stroll to find a letter on the table waiting for him. I had remained indoors all day, for the weather had taken a sudden turn to rain, with high autumnal winds, and the jezail bullet which I had brought back in one of my limbs as a relic of my Afghan campaign, throbbed with dull persistency. With my body in one easy chair and my legs upon another, I had surrounded myself with a cloud of newspapers, until at last, saturated with the news of the day, I tossed them all aside and lay listless, watching the huge crest and monogram upon the envelope upon the table, and wondering lazily who my friend's noble correspondent could be.

'Here is a very fashionable epistle,' I remarked as he entered. 'Your morning's letters, if I remember right, were from a fishmonger and a tide-waiter.'

'Yes, my correspondence has certainly the charm of variety,' he answered, smiling, 'and the humbler are usually the more interesting. This looks like one of those unwelcome social summonses which call upon a man either to be bored or to lie.'

He broke the seal, and glanced over the contents.

'Oh, come, it may prove to be something of interest after all.'

'Not social, then?'

'No, distinctly professional.'

'And from a noble client?'

'One of the highest in England.'

'My dear fellow, I congratulate you.'

'I assure you, Watson, without affectation, that the status of my client is a matter of less moment to me than the interest of his case. It is just possible, however, that that also may not be wanting in this new investigation. You have been reading the papers diligently of late, have you not?'

'It looks like it,' said I ruefully, pointing to a huge bundle in the corner. 'I have had nothing else to do.'

'It is fortunate, for you will perhaps be able to post me up. I read nothing except the criminal news and the agony column. The latter is always instructive. But if you have followed recent events so closely you must have read about Lord St Simon and his wedding?'

'Oh, yes, with the deepest interest.'

'That is well. The letter which I hold in my hand is from Lord St Simon. I will read it to you, and in return you must turn over these papers and let me have whatever bears upon the matter. This is what he says:

My dear Mr Sherlock Holmes,

Lord Backwater tells me that I may place implicit reliance upon your judgement and discretion. I have determined, therefore, to call upon you, and to consult you in reference to the very painful event which has occurred in connection with my wedding. Mr Lestrade, of Scotland Yard, is acting already in the matter, but he assures me that he sees no objection to your co-operation, and that he even thinks that it might be of some assistance. I will call at four o'clock in the afternoon, and should you have any other engagement at that time, I hope you will postpone it, as this is a matter of paramount importance.

Yours faithfully,

ROBERT ST SIMON

'It is dated from Grosvenor Mansions, written

with a quill pen, and the noble lord has had the misfortune to get a smear of ink upon the outer side of his right little finger,' remarked Holmes, as he folded up the epistle.

'He says four o'clock. It is three now. He will be here in an hour.'

'Then I have just time, with your assistance, to get clear upon the subject. Turn over those papers, and arrange the extracts in their order of time, while I take a glance as to who our client is.' He picked a red-covered volume from a line of books of reference beside the mantelpiece. 'Here he is,' said he, sitting down and flattening it out upon his knee. '"Robert Walsingham de Vere St Simon, second son of the Duke of Balmoral" – Hum! "Arms: Azure, three caltrops in chief over a fess sable. Born in 1846." He's forty-one years of age, which is mature for marriage. Was Under-Secretary for the Colonies in a late Administration. The Duke, his father, was at one time Secretary for Foreign Affairs. They inherit Plantagenet blood by direct descent, and Tudor on the distaff side. Ha! Well, there is nothing very instructive in all this. I think I must turn to you, Watson, for something more solid.'

'I have very little difficulty in finding what I want,' said I, 'for the facts are quite recent, and the matter struck me as remarkable. I feared to refer them to you, however, as I knew that you had an inquiry on hand, and that you dislike the intrusion of other matters.'

'Oh, you mean the little problem of the Gros-venor Square furniture van. That is quite cleared up now – though, indeed, it was obvious from the first. Pray give me the results of your newspaper selections.'

'Here is the first notice which I can find. It is in the personal column of the *Morning Post*, and dates, as you see, some weeks back. "A marriage has been arranged," it says, "and will, if rumour is correct, very shortly take place, between Lord Robert St Simon, second son of the Duke of Balmoral, and Miss Hatty Doran, the only daughter of Aloysius Doran, Esq., of San Francisco, Cal., U.S.A." That is all.'

'Terse and to the point,' remarked Holmes, stretching his long thin legs towards the fire.

'There was a paragraph amplifying this in one of the society papers of the same week. Ah, here it is. "There will soon be a call for protection in the marriage market, for the present free trade principle appears to tell heavily against our home product. One by one the management of the noble houses of Great Britain is passing into the hands of our fair cousins from across the Atlantic. An important addition has been made during the last week to the list of prizes which have been borne away by these charming invaders. Lord St Simon, who has shown himself for over twenty years proof against the little god's arrows, has now definitely announced his approaching marriage

with Miss Hatty Doran, the fascinating daughter
of a Californian millionaire. Miss Doran, whose
graceful figure and striking face attracted much
attention at the Westbury House festivities, is
an only child, and it is currently reported that
her dowry will run to considerably over the six
figures, with expectancies for the future. As it is
an open secret that the Duke of Balmoral has
been compelled to sell his pictures within the
last few years, and as Lord St Simon has no
property of his own, save the small estate of
Birchmoor, it is obvious that the Californian heiress is not the only gainer by an alliance which
will enable her to make the easy and common
transition from a Republican lady to a British
title."'

'Anything else?' asked Holmes, yawning.

'Oh yes; plenty. Then there is another note in
the *Morning Post* to say that the marriage would
be an absolutely quiet one, that it would be at St
George's, Hanover Square, that only half-a-dozen
intimate friends would be invited, and that the
party would return to the furnished house at
Lancaster Gate which has been taken by Mr
Aloysius Doran. Two days later – that is, on
Wednesday last – there is a curt announcement
that the wedding had taken place, and that the
honeymoon would be passed at Lord Backwater's
place, near Petersfield. Those are all the notices
which appeared before the disappearance of the
bride.'

'Before the what?' asked Holmes, with a start.

'The vanishing of the lady.'

'When did she vanish, then?'

'At the wedding breakfast.'

'Indeed. This is more interesting than it promised to be; quite dramatic, in fact.'

'Yes; it struck me as being a little out of the common.'

'They often vanish before the ceremony, and occasionally during the honeymoon; but I cannot call to mind anything quite so prompt as this. Pray let me have the details.'

'I warn you that they are very incomplete.'

'Perhaps we may make them less so.'

'Such as they are, they are set forth in a single article of a morning newspaper of yesterday, which I will read to you. It is headed, "Singular Occurrence at a Fashionable Wedding":

'"The family of Lord Robert St Simon has been thrown into the greatest consternation by the strange and painful episodes which have taken place in connection with his wedding. The ceremony, as shortly announced in the papers of yesterday, occurred on the previous morning; but it is only now that it has been possible to confirm the strange rumours which have been so persistently floating about. In spite of the attempts of the friends to hush the matter up, so much public attention has now been drawn to it that no good purpose can be served by affecting to disregard what is a common subject for conversation.

'"The ceremony, which was performed at St George's, Hanover Square, was a very quiet one, no one being present save the father of the bride, Mr Aloysius Doran, the Duchess of Balmoral, Lord Backwater, Lord Eustace and Lady Clara St Simon (the younger brother and sister of the bridegroom), and Lady Alicia Whittington. The whole party proceeded afterwards to the house of Mr Aloysius Doran, at Lancaster Gate, where breakfast had been prepared. It appears that some little trouble had been caused by a woman, whose name has not been ascertained, who endeavoured to force her way into the house after the bridal party, alleging that she had some claim upon Lord St Simon. It was only after a painful and prolonged scene that she was ejected by the butler and the footman. The bride, who had fortunately entered the house before this unpleasant interruption, had sat down to breakfast with the rest, when she complained of a sudden indisposition, and retired to her room. Her prolonged absence having caused some comment, her father followed her; but learned from her maid that she had only come up to her chamber for an instant, caught up an ulster and bonnet, and hurried down to the passage. One of the footmen declared that he had seen a lady leave the house thus apparelled: but had refused to credit that it was his mistress, believing her to be with the company. On ascertaining that his daughter had disappeared, Mr Aloysius Doran, in conjunction with the bridegroom, instantly put themselves into communication with the police, and very energetic inquiries are being made, which will probably result in a speedy clearing up of this very singular business. Up to a late hour last night, however, nothing had transpired as to the whereabouts of the missing lady. There are rumours of foul play in the matter, and it is said that the police have caused the arrest of the woman who had caused the original disturbance, in the belief that, from jealousy or some other motive, she may have been concerned in the strange disappearance of the bride.'''

'And is that all?'

'Only one little item in another of the morning papers, but it is a suggestive one.'

'And it is?'

'That Miss Flora Millar, the lady who had caused the disturbance, has actually been arrested. It appears that she was formerly a *danseuse* at the Allegro, and that she had known the bridegroom for some years. There are no further particulars, and the whole case is in your hands now – so far as it has been set forth in the public press.'

'And an exceedingly interesting case it appears to be. I would not have missed it for worlds. But there is a ring at the bell, Watson, and as the clock makes it a few minutes after four, I have no doubt that this will prove to be our noble client. Do not dream of going, Watson, for I very much prefer having a witness, if only as a check to my own memory.'

'Lord Robert St Simon,' announced our page-boy, throwing open the door. A gentleman entered, with a pleasant, cultured face, high-nosed and pale, with something perhaps of petulance about the mouth, and with the steady, well-opened eye of a man whose pleasant lot it had ever been to command and to be obeyed. His manner was brisk, and yet his general appearance gave an undue impression of age, for he had a slight forward stoop, and a little bend of the knees as he walked. His hair, too as he swept off his curly brimmed hat, was grizzled round the edges, and thin upon the top. As to his dress, it was careful to the verge of foppishness, with high collar, black frock-coat, white waistcoat, yellow gloves, patent-leather shoes, and light-coloured gaiters. He advanced slowly into the room, turning his head from left to right, and swinging in his right hand the cord which held his golden eye-glasses.

'Good day, Lord St Simon,' said Holmes, rising and bowing. 'Pray take the basket chair. This is my friend and colleague, Dr Watson. Draw up a little to the fire, and we shall talk this matter over.'

'A most painful matter to me, as you can most readily imagine, Mr Holmes. I have been cut to the quick. I understand you have already managed several delicate cases of this sort, sir, though I presume that they were hardly from the same class of society.'

'No, I am descending.'

'I beg pardon?'

'My last client of the sort was a king.'

'Oh, really! I had no idea. And which king?'

'The King of Scandinavia.'

'What! Had he lost his wife?'

'You can understand,' said Holmes suavely, 'that I extend to the affairs of my other clients the same secrecy which I promise to you in yours.'

'Of course! Very right! very right! I'm sure I beg pardon. As to my own case, I am ready to give you any information which may assist you in forming an opinion.'

'Thank you. I have already learned all that is in the public prints, nothing more. I presume that I may take it as correct – this article, for example, as to the disappearance of the bride.'

Lord St Simon glanced over it. 'Yes, it is correct, as far as it goes.'

'But it needs a great deal of supplementing before anyone could offer an opinion. I think that I may arrive at my facts most directly by questioning you.'

'Pray do so.'

'When did you first meet Miss Hatty Doran?'

'In San Francisco, a year ago.'

'You were travelling in the States?'

'Yes.'

'Did you become engaged then?'

'No.'

'But you were on a friendly footing?'

'I was amused by her society, and she could see that I was amused.'

'Her father is very rich?'

'He is said to be the richest man on the Pacific Slope.'

'And how did he make his money?'

'In mining. He had nothing a few years ago. Then he struck gold, invested it, and came up by leaps and bounds.'

'Now, what is your own impression as to the young lady's – your wife's character?'

The nobleman swung his glasses a little faster and stared down into the fire. 'You see, Mr Holmes,' said he, 'my wife was twenty before her father became a rich man. During that time she ran free in a mining camp, and wandered through woods or mountains, so that her education has come from nature rather than from the schoolmaster. She is what we call in England a tomboy, with a strong nature, wild and free, unfettered by any sort of traditions. She is impetuous – volcanic, I was about to say. She is swift in making up her mind, and fearless in carrying out her resolutions. On the other hand, I would not have given her the name which I have the honour to bear' (he gave a little stately cough) 'had I not thought her to be at bottom a noble woman. I believe she is capable of heroic self-sacrifice, and that anything dishonourable would be repugnant to her.'

'Have you her photograph?'

'I brought this with me.' He opened a locket,

and showed us the full face of a very lovely woman. It was not a photograph, but an ivory miniature, and the artist had brought out the full effect of the lustrous black hair, the large dark eyes, and the exquisite mouth. Holmes gazed long and earnestly at it. Then he closed the locket and handed it back to Lord St Simon.

'The young lady came to London, then, and you renewed your acquaintance?'

'Yes, her father brought her over for this last London season. I met her several times, became engaged to her, and have now married her.'

'She brought, I understand, a considerable dowry.'

'A fair dowry. Not more than is usual in my family.'

'And this, of course, remains to you, since the marriage is a *fait accompli*?'

'I really have made no inquiries on the subject.'

'Very naturally not. Did you see Miss Doran on the day before the wedding?'

'Yes.'

'Was she in good spirits?'

'Never better. She kept talking of what we should do in our future lives.'

'Indeed. That is very interesting. And on the morning of the wedding?'

'She was as bright as possible – at least, until after the ceremony.'

'And did you observe any change in her then?'

'Well, to tell the truth, I saw then the first signs

that I had ever seen that her temper was just a little sharp. The incident, however, was too trivial to relate, and can have no possible bearing upon the case.'

'Pray let us have it, for all that.'

'Oh, it is childish. She dropped her bouquet as we went towards the vestry. She was passing the front pew at the time, and it fell over into the pew. There was a moment's delay, but the gentleman in the pew handed it up to her again, and it did not appear to be the worse for the fall. Yet, when I spoke to her of the matter, she answered me abruptly; and in the carriage, on our way home, she seemed absurdly agitated over this trifling cause.'

'Indeed. You say that there was a gentleman in the pew. Some of the general public were present, then?'

'Oh, yes. It is impossible to exclude them when the church is open.'

'This gentleman was not one of your wife's friends?'

'No, no; I call him a gentleman by courtesy, but he was quite a common-looking person. I hardly noticed his appearance. But really I think that we are wandering rather far from the point.'

'Lady St Simon, then, returned from the wedding in a less cheerful frame of mind than she had gone to it. What did she do on re-entering her father's house?'

'I saw her in conversation with her maid.'

'And who is her maid?'

'Alice is her name. She is an American, and came from California with her.'

'A confidential servant?'

'A little too much so. It seemed to me that her mistress allowed her to take great liberties. Still, of course, in America they look upon these things in a different way.'

'How long did she speak to this Alice?'

'Oh, a few minutes. I had something else to think of.'

'You did not overhear what they said?'

'Lady St Simon said something about "jumping a claim". She was accustomed to use slang of the kind. I have no idea what she meant.'

'American slang is very expressive sometimes. And what did your wife do when she had finished speaking to her maid?'

'She walked into the breakfast-room.'

'On your arm?'

'No, alone. She was very independent in little matters like that. Then, after we had sat down for ten minutes or so, she rose hurriedly, uttered some words of apology, and left the room. She never came back.'

'But this maid Alice, as I understand, deposes that she went to her room, covered her bride's dress with a long ulster, put on a bonnet, and went out.'

'Quite so. And she was afterwards seen walking into Hyde Park in company with Flora Millar, a woman who is now in custody, and who had already made a disturbance at Mr Doran's house that morning.'

'Ah, yes. I should like a few particulars as to this young lady, and your relations to her.'

Lord St Simon shrugged his shoulders, and raised his eyebrows. 'We have been on a friendly footing for some years – I may say on a *very* friendly footing. She used to be at the Allegro. I have not treated her ungenerously, and she has no just cause of complaint against me, but you know what women are, Mr Holmes. Flora was a dear little thing, but exceedingly hotheaded, and devotedly attached to me. She wrote me dreadful letters when she heard that I was to be married, and to tell the truth the reason why I had the marriage celebrated so quietly was that I feared lest there might be a scandal in the church. She came to Mr Doran's door just after we returned, and she endeavoured to push her way in, uttering very abusive expressions towards my wife, and even threatening her, but I had foreseen the possibility of something of the sort, and I had given instructions to the servants, who soon pushed her out again. She was quiet when she saw that there was no good in making a row.'

'Did your wife hear all this?'

'No, thank goodness, she did not.'

'And she was seen walking with this very woman afterwards?'

'Yes. That is what Mr Lestrade, of Scotland

Yard, looks upon as so serious. It is thought that Flora decoyed my wife out, and laid some terrible trap for her.'

'Well, it is a possible supposition.'

'You think so, too?'

'I did not say a probable one. But you do not yourself look upon this as likely?'

'I do not think Flora would hurt a fly.'

'Still, jealousy is a strange transformer of characters. Pray what is your own theory as to what took place?'

'Well, really, I came to seek a theory, not to propound one. I have given you all the facts. Since you ask me, however, I may say that it has occurred to me as possible that the excitement of this affair, the consciousness that she had made so immense a social stride, had the effect of causing some little nervous disturbance in my wife.'

'In short, that she had become suddenly deranged?'

'Well, really, when I consider that she has turned her back – I will not say upon me, but upon so much that many have aspired to without success – I can hardly explain it in any other fashion.'

'Well, certainly that is also a conceivable hypothesis,' said Holmes, smiling. 'And now, Lord St Simon, I think that I have nearly all my data. May I ask whether you were seated at the breakfast-table so that you could see out of the window?'

'We could see the other side of the road, and the Park.'

'Quite so. Then I do not think that I need detain you any longer. I shall communicate with you.'

'Should you be fortunate enough to solve this problem,' said our client, rising.

'I have solved it.'

'Eh? What was that?'

'I say that I have solved it.'

'Where, then, is my wife?'

'That is a detail which I shall speedily supply.'

Lord St Simon shook his head. 'I am afraid that it will take wiser heads than yours or mine,' he remarked, and bowing in a stately, old-fashioned manner, he departed.

'It is very good of Lord St Simon to honour my head by putting it on a level with his own,' said Sherlock Holmes, laughing. 'I think that I shall have a whisky and soda and a cigar after all this cross-questioning. I had formed my conclusions as to the case before our client came into the room.'

'My dear Holmes!'

'I have notes of several similar cases, though none, as I remarked before, which were quite as prompt. My whole examination served to turn my conjecture into a certainty. Circumstantial evidence is occasionally very convincing, as when you find a trout in the milk, to quote Thoreau's example.'

'But I have heard all that you have heard.'

'Without, however, the knowledge of pre-existing cases which serves me so well. There was a parallel instance in Aberdeen some years back, and something on very much the same lines at Munich the year after the Franco-Prussian War. It is one of these cases – but hullo, here is Lestrade! Good afternoon, Lestrade! You will find an extra tumbler upon the sideboard, and there are cigars in the box.'

The official detective was attired in a pea-jacket and cravat, which gave him a decidedly nautical appearance, and he carried a black canvas bag in his hand. With a short greeting he seated himself, and lit the cigar which had been offered to him.

'What's up, then?' asked Holmes, with a twinkle in his eye. 'You look dissatisfied.'

'And I feel dissatisfied. It is this infernal St Simon marriage case. I can make neither head nor tail of the business.'

'Really! You surprise me.'

'Who ever heard of such a mixed affair? Every clue seems to slip through my fingers. I have been at work upon it all day.'

'And very wet it seems to have made you,' said Holmes, laying his hand upon the arm of the pea-jacket.

'Yes, I have been dragging the Serpentine.'

'In Heaven's name, what for?'

'In search of the body of Lady St Simon.'

Sherlock Holmes leaned back in his chair and laughed heartily.

'Have you dragged the basin of the Trafalgar Square fountain?' he asked.

'Why? What do you mean?'

'Because you have just as good a chance of finding this lady in the one as in the other.'

Lestrade shot an angry glance at my companion. 'I suppose you know all about it,' he snarled.

'Well, I have only just heard the facts, but my mind is made up.'

'Oh, indeed! Then you think that the Serpentine plays no part in the matter?'

'I think it very unlikely.'

'Then perhaps you will kindly explain how it is that we found this in it?' He opened his bag as he spoke, and tumbled on to the floor a wedding dress of watered silk, a pair of white satin shoes, and a bride's wreath and veil, all discoloured and soaked in water. 'There,' said he, putting a new wedding-ring upon the top of the pile. 'There is a little nut for you to crack, Master Holmes.'

'Oh, indeed,' said my friend, blowing blue rings into the air. 'You dragged them from the Serpentine?'

'No. They were found floating near the margin by a park-keeper. They were identified as her clothes, and it seemed to me that if the clothes were there the body would not be far off.'

'By the same brilliant reasoning, every man's body is to be found in the neighbourhood of his wardrobe. And pray what did you hope to arrive at through this?'

'At some evidence implicating Flora Millar in the disappearance.'

'I am afraid you will find it difficult.'

'Are you indeed, now?' cried Lestrade, with some bitterness. 'I am afraid, Holmes, that you are not very practical with your deductions and your inferences. You have made two blunders in as many minutes. This dress does implicate Miss Flora Millar.'

'And how?'

'In the dress is a pocket. In the pocket is a card-case. In the card-case is a note. And here is the very note.' He slapped it down upon the table in front of him. 'Listen to this. "You will see me when all is ready. Come at once, F.H.M." Now my theory all along has been that Lady St Simon was decoyed away by Flora Millar, and that she, with confederates no doubt, was responsible for her disappearance. Here, signed with her initials, is the very note which was no doubt quietly slipped into her hand at the door, and which lured her within their reach.'

'Very good, Lestrade,' said Holmes, laughing. 'You really are very fine indeed. Let me see it.' He took up the paper in a listless way, but his attention instantly became riveted, and he gave a little cry of satisfaction. 'This is indeed important,' said he.

'Ha, you find it so?'

'Extremely so. I congratulate you warmly.'

Lestrade rose in his triumph and bent his head to look. 'Why,' he shrieked, 'you're looking on the wrong side.'

'On the contrary, this is the right side.'

'The right side? You're mad! Here is the note written in pencil over here.'

'And over here is what appears to be a fragment of a hotel bill, which interests me deeply.'

'There's nothing in it. I looked at it before,' said Lestrade. '"Oct. 4th, rooms 8s., breakfast 2s. 6d., cocktail 1s., lunch 2s. 6d., glass sherry 8d." I see nothing in that.'

'Very likely not. It is most important all the same. As to the note, it is important also, or at least the initials are, so I congratulate you again.'

'I've wasted time enough,' said Lestrade, rising, 'I believe in hard work, and not in sitting by the fire spinning fine theories. Good day, Mr Holmes, and we shall see which gets to the bottom of the matter first.' He gathered up the garments, thrust them into the bag, and made for the door.

'Just one hint to you, Lestrade,' drawled Holmes, before his rival vanished; 'I will tell you the true solution of the matter. Lady St Simon is a myth. There is not, and there never has been, any such person.'

Lestrade looked sadly at my companion. Then he turned to me, tapped his forehead three times, shook his head solemnly, and hurried away.

He had hardly shut the door behind him, when

Holmes rose and put on his overcoat. 'There is something in what the fellow says about outdoor work,' he remarked, 'so I think, Watson, that I must leave you to your papers for a little.'

It was after five o'clock when Sherlock Holmes left me, but I had no time to be lonely, for within an hour there arrived a confectioner's man with a very large flat box. This he unpacked with the help of a youth whom he had brought with him, and presently, to my very great astonishment, a quite epicurean little cold supper began to be laid out upon our humble lodging-house mahogany. There were a couple of brace of cold woodcock, a pheasant, a *pâté de foie gras* pie, with a group of ancient and cobwebby bottles. Having laid out all these luxuries, my two visitors vanished away, like the genii of the Arabian Nights, with no explanation save that the things had been paid for and were ordered to this address.

Just before nine o'clock Sherlock Holmes stepped briskly into the room. His features were gravely set, but there was a light in his eye which made me think that he had not been disappointed in his conclusions.

'They have laid the supper, then,' he said, rubbing his hands.

'You seem to expect company. They have laid for five.'

'Yes, I fancy we may have some company dropping in,' said he. 'I am surprised that Lord St

Simon has not already arrived. Ha! I fancy that I hear his step now upon the stairs.'

It was indeed our visitor of the morning who came bustling in, dangling his glasses more vigorously than ever, and with a very perturbed expression upon his aristocratic features.

'My message reached you, then?' asked Holmes.

'Yes, and I must confess that the contents startled me beyond measure. Have you good authority for what you say?'

'The best possible.'

Lord St Simon sank into a chair, and passed his hand over his forehead.

'What will the Duke say,' he murmured, 'when he hears that one of the family has been subjected to such a humiliation?'

'It is the purest accident. I cannot allow that there is humiliation.'

'Ah, you look on these things from another standpoint.'

'I fail to see that anyone is to blame. I can hardly see how the lady could have acted otherwise, though her abrupt method of doing it was undoubtedly to be regretted. Having no other, she had no one to advise her at such a crisis.'

'It was a slight, sir, a public slight,' said Lord St Simon, tapping his fingers upon the table.

'You must make allowance for this poor girl, placed in so unprecedented a position.'

'I will make no allowance. I am very angry indeed, and I have been shamefully used.'

'I think I heard a ring,' said Holmes. 'Yes, there are steps on the landing. If I cannot persuade you to take a lenient view of the matter, Lord St Simon, I have brought an advocate here who may be more successful.' He opened the door and ushered in a lady and gentleman. 'Lord St Simon,' said he, 'allow me to introduce you to Mr and Mrs Francis Hay Moulton. The lady, I think, you have already met.'

At the sight of these newcomers our client had sprung from his seat, and stood very erect, with his eyes cast down and his hand thrust into the breast of his frock-coat, a picture of offended dignity. The lady had taken a quick step forward and had held out her hand to him, but he still refused to raise his eyes. It was as well for his resolution, perhaps, for her pleading face was one which it was hard to resist.

'You're angry, Robert,' said she. 'Well, I guess you have every cause to be.'

'Pray make no apology to me,' said Lord St Simon bitterly.

'Oh, yes, I know that I treated you real bad, and that I should have spoken to you before I went; but I was kind of rattled, and from the time when I saw Frank here again, I just didn't know what I was doing or saying. I only wonder that I didn't fall down and do a faint right there before the altar.'

'Perhaps, Mrs Moulton, you would like my friend and me to leave the room while you explain this matter?'

'If I may give an opinion,' remarked the strange gentleman, 'we've had just a little too much secrecy over this business already. For my part, I should like all Europe and America to hear the rights of it.' He was a small, wiry, sunburned man, with a sharp face and alert manner.

'Then I'll tell our story right away,' said the lady. 'Frank here and I met in '81, in McQuire's camp, near the Rockies, where Pa was working a claim. We were engaged to each other, Frank and I; but then one day Pa rather struck a rich pocket, and made a pile, while poor Frank here had a claim that petered out and came to nothing. The richer Pa grew, the poorer was Frank; so at last Pa wouldn't hear of our engagement lasting any longer, and he took me away to 'Frisco. Frank wouldn't throw up his hand, though; so he followed me there, and he saw me without Pa knowing anything about it. It would only have made him mad to know, so we just fixed it all up for ourselves. Frank said that he would go and make his pile, too, and never come back to claim me until he had as much as Pa. So then I promised to wait for him to the end of time, and pledged myself not to marry anyone else while he lived. "Why shouldn't we be married right away, then," said he, "and then I will feel sure of you; and I won't claim to be your husband until I come back." Well, we talked it over, and he had fixed it all up so nicely, with a clergyman all ready in waiting, that we just did it right there; and then

Frank went off to seek his fortune and I went back to Pa.

'The next that I heard of Frank was that he was in Montana, and then he went prospecting into Arizona, and then I heard of him from New Mexico. After that came a long newspaper story about how a miners' camp had been attacked by Apache Indians, and there was my Frank's name among the killed. I fainted dead away, and I was very sick for months after. Pa thought I had a decline, and took me to half the doctors in 'Frisco. Not a word of news came for a year or more, so that I never doubted that Frank was really dead. Then Lord St Simon came to 'Frisco, and we came to London, and a marriage was arranged, and Pa was very pleased, but I felt all the time that no man on this earth would ever take the place in my heart that had been given to my poor Frank.

'Still, if I had married Lord St Simon, of course I'd have done my duty by him. We can't command our love, but we can our actions. I went to the altar with him with the intention that I would make him just as good a wife as it was in me to be. But you may imagine what I felt when, just as I came to the altar rails, I glanced and saw Frank standing looking at me out of the first pew. I thought it was his ghost at first; but, when I looked again, there he was still, with a kind of question in his eyes as if to ask me whether I were glad or sorry to see him. I wonder I didn't drop. I know that everything was turning round, and the words of the clergyman were just like the buzz of a bee in my ear. I didn't know what to do. Should I stop the service and make a scene in the church? I glanced at him again, and he seemed to know what I was thinking, for he raised his finger to his lips to tell me to be still. Then I saw him scribble on a piece of paper, and I knew he was writing me a note. As I passed his pew on the way out I dropped my bouquet over to him, and he slipped the note into my hand when he returned me the flowers. It was only a line asking me to join him when he made the sign to me to do so. Of course I never doubted for a moment that my first duty was now to him, and I determined to do just whatever he might direct.

'When I got back I told my maid, who had known him in California, and had always been his friend. I ordered her to say nothing, but to get a few things packed and my ulster ready. I know I ought to have spoken to Lord St Simon, but it was dreadful hard before his mother and all those great people. I just made up my mind to run away, and explain afterwards. I hadn't been at the table ten minutes before I saw Frank out of the window at the other side of the road. He beckoned to me, and then began walking into the Park. I slipped out, put on my things, and followed him. Some woman came talking something or other about Lord St Simon to me – seemed to me from the little I heard as if he had a little secret of his own before marriage also – but I managed to get away from her, and soon overtook Frank. We got into a cab together, and away we drove to some lodgings he had taken in Gordon Square, and that was my true wedding after all those years of waiting. Frank had been a prisoner among the Apaches, had escaped, came on to 'Frisco, found that I had given him up for dead and had gone to England, followed me there, and had come upon me at last on the very morning of my second wedding.'

'I saw it in a paper,' explained the American. 'It gave the name and the church, but not where the lady lived.'

'Then we had a talk as to what we should do, and Frank was all for openness, but I was so ashamed of it all that I felt as if I would like to vanish away and never see any of them again, just sending a line to Pa, perhaps, to show him that I was alive. It was awful of me to think of all those lords and ladies sitting round that breakfast-table, and waiting for me to come back. So Frank took my wedding clothes and things, and made a bundle of them so that I should not be traced, and dropped them away somewhere where no one should find them. It is likely that we should have gone on to Paris tomorrow, only that this good gentleman, Mr Holmes, came round to us this evening, though how he found us is more than I can think, and he showed us very clearly and kindly that I was wrong and that Frank was right, and that we should put ourselves in the wrong if we were so secret. Then he offered to give us a chance of talking to Lord St Simon alone, and so we came right away and I am very sorry if I have given you pain, and I hope that you do not think very meanly of me.'

Lord St Simon had by no means relaxed his rigid attitude, but had listened with a frowning brow and a compressed lip to this long narrative.

'Excuse me,' he said, 'but it is not my custom to discuss most intimate personal affairs in this public manner.'

'Then you won't forgive me? You won't shake hands before I go?'

'Oh, certainly, if it would give you any pleasure.' He put out his hand and coldly grasped that which she extended to him.

'I had hoped,' suggested Holmes, 'that you would have joined us in a friendly supper.'

'I think that there you ask a little too much,' responded his lordship. 'I may be forced to acquiesce in these recent developments, but I can hardly be expected to make merry over them. I think that, with your permission, I will now wish you all a very good night.' He included us all in a sweeping bow, and stalked out of the room.

'Then I trust that you at least will honour me with your company,' said Sherlock Holmes. 'It is always a joy to me to meet an American, Mr Moulton, for I am one of those who believe that the folly of a monarch and the blundering of a

Minister in fargone years will not prevent our children from being some day citizens of the same world-wide country under a flag which shall be a quartering of the Union Jack with the Stars and Stripes.'

'The case has been an interesting one,' remarked Holmes, when our visitors had left, 'because it serves to show very clearly how simple the explanation may be of an affair which at first sight seems to be almost explicable. Nothing could be more inexplicable. Nothing could be more natural than the sequence of events as narrated by this lady, and nothing stranger than the result when viewed, for instance, by Mr Lestrade of Scotland Yard.'

'You were not yourself at fault, then?'

'From the first, two facts were very obvious to me, the one that the lady had been quite willing to undergo the wedding ceremony, the other that she had repented of it within a few minutes of returning home. Obviously something had occurred during the morning, then, to cause her to change her mind. What could that something be? She could not have spoken to anyone when she was out, for she had been in the company of the bridegroom. Had she seen someone, then? If she had, it must be someone from America, because she had spent so short a time in this country that she could hardly have allowed anyone to acquire so deep an influence over her that the mere sight of him would induce her to change her plans so completely. You see we have already arrived, by a process of exclusion, at the idea that she might have seen an American. Then who could this American be, and why should he possess so much influence over her? It might be a lover; it might be a husband. Her young womanhood had, I knew, been spent in rough scenes, and under strange conditions. So far had I got before I ever heard Lord St Simon's narrative. When he told us of a man in a pew, of the change in the bride's manner, of so transparent a device of obtaining a note as the dropping of a bouquet, of her resort to her confidential maid, and of her very significant allusion to claim-jumping, which in miners' parlance means taking possession of that which another person has prior claim to, the whole situation became absolutely clear. She had gone off with a man, and the man was either a lover or was a previous husband, the chances being in favour of the latter.'

'And how in the world did you find them?'

'It might have been difficult, but friend Lestrade held information in his hands the value of which he did not himself know. The initials were of course of the highest importance, but more valuable still was it to know that within a week he had settled his bill at one of the most select London hotels.'

'How did you deduce the select?'

'By the select prices. Eight shillings for a bed and eight-pence for a glass of sherry, pointed to one of the most expensive hotels. There are not many in London which charge at that rate. In the second one which I visited in Northumberland Avenue, I learned by an inspection of the book that Francis H. Moulton, an American gentleman, had left only the day before, and on looking over the entries against him, I came upon the very items which I had seen in the duplicate bill. His letters were to be forwarded to 226 Gordon Square, so thither I travelled, and being fortunate enough to find the loving couple at home, I ventured to give them some paternal advice, and to point out to them that it would be better in every way that they should make their position a little clearer, both to the general public and to Lord St Simon in particular. I invited them to meet him here, and, as you see, I made him keep the appointment.'

'But with no very good results,' I remarked. 'His conduct was certainly not very gracious.'

'Ah! Watson,' said Holmes, smiling, 'perhaps you would not be very gracious either, if, after all the trouble of wooing and wedding, you found yourself deprived in an instant of wife and of fortune. I think that we may judge Lord St Simon very mercifully, and thank our stars that we are never likely to find ourselves in the same position. Draw your chair up, and hand me my violin, for the only problem which we have still to solve is how to while away these bleak autumnal evenings.'

THE CROOKED MAN

One summer night, a few months after my marriage, I was seated by my own hearth smoking a last pipe and nodding over a novel, for my day's work had been an exhausting one. My wife had already gone upstairs, and the sound of the locking of the door some time before told me that the servants had also retired. I had risen from my seat and was knocking out the ashes of my pipe, when I suddenly heard the clang of the bell.

I looked at the clock. It was a quarter to twelve. This could not be a visitor at so late an hour. A patient, evidently, and possibly an all-night sitting. With a wry face I went out into the hall and opened the door. To my astonishment, it was Sherlock Holmes who stood upon my step.

'Ah, Watson,' said he, 'I hoped that I might not be too late to catch you.'

'My dear fellow, pray come in.'

'You look surprised, and no wonder! Relieved, too, I fancy! Hum! you still smoke the Arcadia mixture of your bachelor days, then! There's no mistaking that fluffy ash upon your coat. It's easy to tell that you've been accustomed to wear a uniform, Watson; you'll never pass as a pure-bred civilian as long as you keep that habit of carrying your handkerchief in your sleeve. Could you put me up tonight?'

'With pleasure.'

'You told me that you had bachelor quarters for one, and I see that you have no gentleman visitor at present. Your hat-stand proclaims as much.'

'I shall be delighted if you will stay.'

'Thank you. I'll find a vacant peg, then. Sorry to see that you've had the British workman in the house. He's a token of evil. Not the drains, I hope?'

'No, the gas.'

'Ah! He has left two nail marks from his boot upon your linoleum just where the light strikes it. No, thank you, I had some supper at Waterloo, but I'll smoke a pipe with you with pleasure.'

I handed him my pouch, and he seated himself opposite to me, and smoked for some time in silence. I was well aware that nothing but business of importance could have brought him to me at such an hour, so I waited patiently until he should come round to it.

'I see that you are professionally rather busy just now,' said he, glancing keenly across at me.

'Yes, I've had a busy day,' I answered. 'It may seem very foolish in your eyes,' I added, 'but really I don't know how you deduced it.'

Holmes chuckled to himself.

'I have the advantage of knowing your habits,

my dear Watson,' said he. 'When your round is a short one you walk, and when it is a long one you use a hansom. As I perceive that your boots, although used, are by no means dirty, I cannot doubt that you are at present busy enough to justify the hansom.'

'Excellent!' I cried.

'Elementary,' said he. 'It is one of those instances where the reasoner can produce an effect which seems remarkable to his neighbour, because the latter has missed the one little point which is the basis of the deduction. The same may be said, my dear fellow, for the effect of some of these little sketches of yours, which is entirely meretricious, depending as it does upon your retaining in your own hands some factors in the problem which are never imparted to the reader. Now, at present I am in the position of these same readers, for I hold in this hand several threads of one of the strangest cases which ever perplexed a man's brain, and yet I lack the one or two which are needful to complete my theory. But I'll have them, Watson, I'll have them!' His eyes kindled and a slight flush sprang into his thin cheeks. For an instant the veil had lifted upon his keen, intense nature, but for an instant only. When I glanced again his face had resumed that Red Indian composure which had made so many regard him as a machine rather than a man.

'The problem presents features of interest,' said he; 'I may even say very exceptional features of interest. I have already looked into the matter, and have come, as I think, within sight of my solution. If you could accompany me in that last step, you might be of considerable service to me.'

'I should be delighted.'

'Could you go as far as Aldershot tomorrow?'

'I have no doubt Jackson would take my practice.'

'Very good. I want to start by the 11.10 from Waterloo.'

'That would give me time.'

'Then, if you are not sleepy, I will give you a sketch of what has happened and of what remains to be done.'

'I was sleepy before you came. I am quite wakeful now.'

'I will compress the story as far as may be done without omitting anything vital to the case. It is conceivable that you may even have read some account of the matter. It is the supposed murder of Colonel Barclay, of the Royal Mallows, at Aldershot, which I am investigating.'

'I have heard nothing of it.'

'It has not excited much attention yet, except locally. The facts are only two days old. Briefly they are these:

'The Royal Mallows is, as you know, one of the most famous Irish regiments in the British Army. It did wonders both in the Crimea and the Mutiny, and has since that time distinguished itself upon every possible occasion. It was commanded up to Monday night by James Barclay, a gallant veteran, who started as a full private, was raised to commissioned rank for his bravery at the time of the Mutiny, and so lived to command the regiment in which he had once carried a musket.

'Colonel Barclay had married at the time when he was a sergeant, and his wife, whose maiden name was Miss Nancy Devoy, was the daughter of a former colour-sergeant in the same corps. There was, therefore, as can be imagined some little social friction when the young couple (for they were still young) found themselves in their new surroundings. They appear, however, to have quickly adapted themselves, and Mrs Barclay has always, I understand, been as popular with the ladies of the regiment as her husband was with his brother officers. I may add that she was a woman of great beauty, and that even now, when she has been married for upwards of thirty years, she is still of a striking appearance.

'Colonel Barclay's family life appears to have been a uniformly happy one. Major Murphy, to whom I owe most of my facts, assures me that he has never heard of any misunderstanding between the pair. On the whole he thinks that Barclay's devotion to his wife was greater than his wife's to Barclay. He was acutely uneasy if he were absent from her for a day. She, on the other hand, though devoted and faithful, was less obtrusively affectionate. But they were regarded in the regiment as the very model of a middle-aged couple. There was absolutely nothing in their mutual relations to prepare people for the tragedy which was to follow.

'Colonel Barclay himself seems to have had some singular traits in his character. He was a dashing, jovial old soldier in his usual mood, but there were occasions on which he seemed to show himself capable of considerable violence and vindictiveness. This side of his nature, however, appears never to have been turned towards his wife. Another fact which had struck Major Murphy, and three out of five of the other officers with whom I conversed, was the singular sort of depression which came upon him at times. As the Major expressed it, the smile had often been struck from his mouth, as if by some invisible hand, when he had been joining in the gaieties and chaff of the mess table. For days on end, when the mood was on him, he had been sunk in the deepest gloom. This and a certain tinge of superstition were the only unusual traits in his character which his brother officers had observed. The latter peculiarity took the form of a dislike of being left alone, especially after dark. This puerile feature in a nature which was conspicuously manly had often given rise to comment and conjecture.

'The first battalion of the Royal Mallows (which is the old 117th) has been stationed at Aldershot for some years. The married officers live out of barracks, and the Colonel has during all this time occupied a villa called Lachine, about half a mile from the North Camp. The house stands in its own grounds, but the west side of it is not more than thirty yards from the high road. A coachman and two maids form the staff of servants. These, with their master and mistress, were the sole occupants of Lachine, for the Barclays had no children, nor was it usual for them to have resident visitors.

'Now for the events at Lachine between nine and ten on the evening of last Monday.

'Mrs Barclay was, it appears, a member of the Roman Catholic Church, and had interested herself very much in the establishment of the Guild of St George, which was formed in connexion with the Watt Street Chapel for the purpose of supplying the poor with cast-off clothing. A meeting of the Guild had been held that evening at eight, and Mrs Barclay had hurried over her dinner in order to be present at it. When leaving the house, she was heard by the coachman to make some commonplace remark to her husband, and to assure him that she would be back before long. She then called for Miss Morrison, a young lady who lives in the next villa, and the two went off together to their meeting. It lasted forty minutes, and at a quarter past nine Mrs Barclay returned home, having left Miss Morrison at her door as she passed.

'There is a room which is used as a morning-room at Lachine. This faces the road, and opens by a large glass folding door on to the lawn. The lawn is thirty yards across, and is only divided from the highway by a low wall with an iron rail above it. It was into this room that Mrs Barclay went upon her return. The blinds were not down, for the room was seldom used in the evening, but Mrs Barclay herself lit the lamp and then rang the bell, asking Jane Stewart, the housemaid, to bring her a cup of tea, which was quite contrary to her usual habits. The Colonel had been sitting in the dining-room, but hearing that his wife had returned, he joined her in the morning-room. The coachman saw him cross the hall, and enter it. He was never seen again alive.

'The tea which had been ordered was brought up at the end of ten minutes, but the maid, as she approached the door, was surprised to hear the voices of her master and mistress in furious altercation. She knocked without receiving any answer, and even turned the handle, but only to find that the door was locked upon the inside. Naturally enough, she ran down to tell the cook, and the two women with the coachman came up into the hall and listened to the dispute which was still raging. They all agree that only two voices were to be heard, those of Barclay and his wife. Barclay's remarks were subdued and abrupt, so that none of them were audible to the listeners. The lady's, on the other hand, were most bitter, and, when she raised her voice, could be plainly heard. "You coward!" she repeated over and over again. "What can be done now? Give me back my life. I will never so much as breathe the same air as you again! You coward! You coward!" Those were scraps of her conversation, ending in a sudden dreadful cry in the man's voice, with a crash, and a piercing scream from the woman. Convinced that some tragedy had occurred, the coachman rushed to the door and strove to force it, while scream after scream issued from within. He was unable, however, to make his way in, and the maids were too distracted with fear to be of any assistance to him. A sudden thought struck him, however, and he ran through the hall door and round to the lawn, upon which the long french windows opened. One side of the window was open, which I understand was quite usual in the summer-time, and he passed without difficulty into the room. His mistress had ceased to scream, and was stretched insensible upon a couch, while with his feet tilted over the side of an armchair, and his head upon the ground near the corner of the fender, was lying the unfortunate soldier, stone dead, in a pool of his own blood.

'Naturally the coachman's first thought, on finding that he could do nothing for his master, was to open the door. But here an unexpected and singular difficulty presented itself. The key was not on the inner side of the door, nor could he find it anywhere in the room. He went out again, therefore, through the window, and having obtained the help of a policeman and of a medical man, he returned. The lady, against whom naturally the strongest suspicion rested, was removed to her room, still in a state of insensibility. The Colonel's body was then placed upon the sofa, and a careful examination made of the scene of the tragedy.

'The injury from which the unfortunate veteran was suffering was found to be a ragged cut, some two inches long, at the back part of his head, which had evidently been caused by a violent blow from a blunt weapon. Nor was it difficult to guess what that weapon may have been. Upon the floor, close to the body, was lying a singular club of hard carved wood with a bone handle. The Colonel possessed a varied collection of weapons brought from the different countries in which he had fought, and it is conjectured by the police that this club was among his trophies. The servants deny having seen it before, but among the numerous curiosities in the house it is possible that it may have been overlooked. Nothing else of importance was discovered in the room by the police, save the inexplicable fact that neither upon Mrs Barclay's person, nor upon that of the victim, nor in any part of the room was the missing key to be found. The door had eventually to be opened by a locksmith from Aldershot.

'That was the state of things, Watson, when upon the Tuesday morning I, at the request of Major Murphy, went down to Aldershot to supplement the efforts of the police. I think you will acknowledge that the problem was already one of interest, but my observations soon made me realize that it was in truth much more extraordinary than would at first sight appear.

'Before examining the room I cross-questioned the servants, but only succeeded in eliciting the facts which I have already stated. One other detail of interest was remembered by Jane Stewart, the housemaid. You will remember that on hearing the sound of the quarrel she descended and returned with the other servants. On that first occasion, when she was alone, she says that the voices of her master and mistress were sunk so low that she could hear hardly anything, and judged by their tones, rather than their words, that they had fallen out. On my pressing her, however, she remembered that she heard the word "David" uttered twice by the lady. The point is of the utmost importance as guiding us towards the reason of the sudden quarrel. The Colonel's name, you remember, was James.

'There was one thing in the case which had made the deepest impression both upon the servants and the police. This was the contortion of the Colonel's face. It had set, according to their account, into the most dreadful expression of fear and horror which a human countenance is capable of assuming. More than one person fainted at the mere sight of him, so terrible was the effect. It was quite certain that he had foreseen his fate, and that it had caused him the utmost horror. This, of course, fitted in well enough with the police theory, if the Colonel could have seen his wife making a murderous attack upon him. Nor was the fact of the wound being on the back of his head a fatal objection to this, as he might have turned to avoid the blow. No information could be got from the lády herself, who was temporarily insane from an acute attack of brain fever.

'From the police I learned that Miss Morrison, who, you remember, went out that evening with Mrs Barclay, denied having any knowledge of what it was which had caused the ill-humour in which her companion had returned.

'Having gathered these facts, Watson, I smoked several pipes over them, trying to separate those which were crucial from others which were merely incidental. There could be no question that the most distinctive and suggestive point in the case was the singular disappearance of the door key. A most careful search had failed to discover it in the room. Therefore, it must have been taken from it. But neither the Colonel nor the Colonel's wife could have taken it. That was perfectly clear. Therefore a third person must have entered the room. And that third person could only have come through the window. It seemed to me that a careful examination of the room and the lawn might possibly reveal some traces of this mysteri-ous individual. You know my methods, Watson. There was not one of them which I did not apply to the inquiry. And it ended by my discovering traces, but very different ones from those which I had expected. There had been a man in the room, and he had crossed the lawn coming from the road. I was able to obtain five very clear impressions of his footmarks – one on the roadway itself, at the point where he had climbed the low wall, two on the lawn, and two very faint ones upon the stained boards near the window where he had entered. He had apparently rushed across the lawn, for his toe marks were much deeper that his heels. But it was not the man who surprised me. It was his companion.'

'His companion!'

Holmes pulled a large sheet of tissue paper out of his pocket and carefully unfolded it upon his knee.

'What do you make of that?' he asked.

The paper was covered with tracings of the footmarks some small animal. It had five well-marked footpads, an indication of long nails, and the whole print might be nearly as large as a dessert spoon.

'It's a dog,' said I.

'Did you ever hear of a dog running up a curtain? I found distinct traces that this creature had done so.'

'A monkey, then?'

'But it is not the print of a monkey.'

'What can it be, then?'

'Neither dog, nor cat, nor monkey, nor any creature that we are familiar with. I have tried to reconstruct it from the measurements. Here are four prints where the beast has been standing motionless. You see that it is no less than fifteen inches from fore foot to hind. Add to that the length of neck and head, and you get a creature not much less than two feet long – probably more if there is any tail. But now observe this other measurement. The animal has been moving, and we have the length of its stride. In each case it is only about three inches. You have an indication, you see, of a long body with very short legs attached to it. It has not been considerate enough to leave any of its hair behind it. But its general shape must be what I have indicated, and it can run up a curtain and is carnivorous.'

'How do you deduce that?'

'Because it ran up the curtain. A canary's cage was hanging in the window, and its aim seems to have been to get at the bird.'

'Then what was the beast?'

'Ah, if I could give it a name it might go a long way towards solving the case. On the whole it was probably some creature of the weasel or stoat tribe – and yet it is larger than any of these that I have seen.'

'But what had it to do with the crime?'

'That also is still obscure. But we have learned a good deal, you perceive. We know that a man stood in the road looking at the quarrel between the Barclays – the blinds were up and the room lighted. We know also that he ran across the lawn, entered the room, accompanied by a strange animal, and that he either struck the Colonel, or, as is equally possible, that the Colonel fell down from sheer fright at the sight of him, and cut his head on the corner of the fender. Finally, we have the curious fact that the intruder carried away the key with him when he left.'

'Your discoveries seem to have left the business more obscure than it was before,' said I.

'Quite so. They undoubtedly showed that the affair was much deeper than was at first conjectured. I thought the matter over, and I came to the conclusion that I must approach the case from another aspect. But really, Watson, I am keeping you up, and I might just as well tell you all this on our way to Aldershot tomorrow.'

'Thank you, you've gone rather too far to stop.'

'It was quite certain that when Mrs Barclay left the house at half past seven she was on good terms with her husband. She was never, as I think I have said, ostentatiously affectionate, but she was heard by the coachman chatting with the Colonel in a friendly fashion. Now, it was equally certain that immediately on her return she had gone to the room in which she was least likely to see her husband, had flown to tea, as an agitated woman will, and, finally, on his coming in to her, had broken into violent recriminations. Therefore, something had occurred between seven-thirty and nine o'clock which had completely altered her feelings towards him. But Miss Morrison had been with her during the whole of that hour and a half. It was absolutely certain, therefore, in spite of her denial, that she must know something of the matter.

'My first conjecture was that possibly there had been some passages between this young woman and the old soldier, which the former had now confessed to the wife. That would account for the angry return and also for the girl's denial that anything had occurred. Nor would it be entirely incompatible with most of the words overheard. But there was the reference to David, and there was the known affection of the Colonel for his wife to weigh against it, to say nothing of the tragic intrusion of this other man, which might, of course, be entirely disconnected with what had gone before. It was not easy to pick one's steps, but on the whole I was inclined to dismiss the idea that there had been anything between the Colonel and Miss Morrison, but more than ever convinced that the young lady held the clue as to what it was which had turned Mrs Barclay to hatred of her husband. I took the obvious course, therefore, of calling upon Miss Morrison, of explaining to her that I was perfectly certain that she held the facts in her possession, and of assuring her that her friend, Mrs Barclay, might find herself in the dock upon a capital charge unless the matter were cleared up.

'Miss Morrison is a little, ethereal slip of a girl, with timid eyes and blonde hair, but I found her by no means wanting in shrewdness and common sense. She sat thinking for some time after I had spoken, and then turning to me with a brisk air of resolution, she broke into a remarkable statement, which I will condense for your benefit.

'"I promised my friend that I would say nothing of the matter, and a promise is a promise," said she. "But if I can really help her when so serious a charge is made against her, and when her own mouth, poor darling, is closed by illness, then I think I am absolved from my promise. I will tell you exactly what happened on Monday evening.

'"We were returning from the Watt Street Mission, about a quarter to nine o'clock. On our way we had to pass through Hudson Street, which is a very quiet thoroughfare. There is only one lamp in it upon the left-hand side, and as we approached this lamp I saw a man coming towards us with his back very bent, and something like a box slung over one of his shoulders. He appeared to be deformed, for he carried his head low, and walked with his knees bent. We were passing him when he raised his face to look at us in the circle of light thrown by the lamp, and as he did so he stopped and screamed out in a dreadful voice, 'My God, it's Nancy!' Mrs Barclay turned as white as death, and would have fallen down had the dreadful-looking creature not caught hold of her. I was going to call for the police, but she, to my surprise, spoke quite civilly to the fellow.

'"'I thought you had been dead this thirty years, Henry,' said she, in a shaking voice.

"'"So I have,' said he and it was awful to hear the tones that he said it in. He had a very dark, fearsome face, and a gleam in his eyes that comes back to me in my dreams. His hair and whiskers were shot with grey, and his face was all crinkled and puckered like a withered apple.

"'"Just walk on a little way, dear,' said Mrs Barclay. 'I want to have a word with this man. There is nothing to be afraid of.' She tried to speak boldly, but she was still deadly pale, and could hardly get her words out for the trembling of her lips.

"'"I did as she asked me, and they talked together for a few minutes. Then she came down the street with her eyes blazing, and I saw the crippled wretch standing by the lamp-post and shaking his clenched fists in the air, as if he were mad with rage. She never said a word until we were at the door here, when she took me by the hand and begged me to tell no one what had happened. 'It is an old acquaintance of mine who has come down in the world,' said she. When I promised her that I would say nothing she kissed me, and I have never seen her since. I have told you now the whole truth, and if I withheld it from the police it is because I did not realize then the danger in which my dear friend stood. I know that it can only be to her advantage that everything should be known.'"

'There was her statement, Watson, and to me, as you can imagine, it was like a light on a dark night. Everything which had been disconnected before began at once to assume its true place, and I had a shadowy presentiment of the whole sequence of events. My next step obviously was to find the man who had produced such a remarkable impression upon Mrs Barclay. If he were still in Aldershot it should not be a very difficult matter. There are not such a very great number of civilians, and a deformed man was sure to have attracted attention. I spent a day in the search, and by evening – this very evening, Watson – I had run him down. The man's name is Henry Wood, and he lives in lodgings in the same street in which the ladies met him. He has only been five days in the place. In the character of a registration agent I had a most interesting gossip with his landlady. The man is by trade a conjurer and performer, going round the canteens, after nightfall, and giving a little entertainment at each. He carries some creature about with him in his box, about which the landlady seemed to be in considerable trepidation, for she had never seen an animal like it. He uses it in some of his tricks, according to her account. So much the woman was able to tell me, and also that it was a wonder the man lived, seeing how twisted he was, and that he spoke in a strange tongue sometimes, and that for the last two nights she had heard him groaning and weeping in his bedroom. He was all right as far as money went, but in his deposit he had given her what looked like a bad florin. She showed it to me, Watson, and it was an Indian rupee.

'So now, my dear fellow, you see exactly how we stand and why it is I want you. It is perfectly plain that after the ladies parted from this man he followed them at a distance, that he saw the quarrel between husband and wife through the window, that he rushed in, and that the creature which he carried in his box got loose. That is all very certain. But he is the only person in this world who can tell us exactly what happened in that room.'

'And you intend to ask him?'

'Most certainly – but in the presence of a witness.'

'And I am the witness?'

'If you will be so good. If he can clear the matter up, well and good. If he refuses, we have no alternative but to apply for a warrant.'

'But how do you know he will be there when we return?'

'You may be sure that I took some precautions. I have one of my Baker Street boys mounting guard over him who would stick to him like a burr, go where he might. We shall find him in Hudson Street tomorrow, Watson; and meanwhile I should be the criminal myself if I kept you out of bed any longer.'

It was midday when we found ourselves at the scene of the tragedy, and, under my companion's guidance, we made our way at once to Hudson Street. In spite of his capacity for concealing his emotions I could easily see that Holmes was in a state of suppressed excitement, while I was myself tingling with that half-sporting, half-intellectual pleasure which I invariably experienced when I associated myself with him in his investigations.

'This is the street,' said he, as he turned into a short thoroughfare lined with plain, two-storeyed brick houses – 'Ah! here is Simpson to report.'

'He's in all right, Mr Holmes,' cried a small street Arab, running up to us.

'Good, Simpson!' said Holmes, patting him on the head. 'Come along, Watson. This is the house.' He sent in his card with a message that he had come on important business, and a moment later we were face to face with the man whom we had come to see. In spite of the warm weather he was crouching over a fire and the little room was like an oven. The man sat all twisted and huddled in his chair in a way which gave an indescribable impression of deformity, but the face which he turned towards us, though worn and swarthy, must at some time have been remarkable for its beauty. He looked suspiciously at us now out of yellow-shot bilious eyes, and, without speaking or rising, he waved towards two chairs.

'Mr Henry Wood, late of India, I believe?' said Holmes, affably. 'I've come over this little matter of Colonel Barclay's death.'

'What should I know about that?'

'That's what I wanted to ascertain. You know, I suppose, that unless the matter is cleared up,

Mrs Barclay, who is an old friend of yours, will in all probability be tried for murder?'

The man gave a violent start.

'I don't know who you are,' he cried, 'nor how you come to know what you do know, but will you swear that this is true that you tell me?'

'Why, they are only waiting for her to come to her senses to arrest her.'

'My God! Are you in the police yourself?'

'No.'

'What business is it of yours, then?'

'It's every man's business to see justice done.'

'You can take my word that she is innocent.'

'Then you are guilty?'

'No, I am not.'

'Who killed Colonel James Barclay, then?'

'It was a just Providence that killed him. But mind you this, that if I had knocked his brains out, as it was in my heart to do, he would have had no more than his due from my hands. If his own guilty conscience had not struck him down, it is likely enough that I might have had his blood upon my soul. You want me to tell the story? Well, I don't know why I shouldn't, for there's no cause for me to be ashamed of it.

'It was in this way, sir. You see me now with my back like a camel and my ribs all awry, but there was a time when Corporal Henry Wood was the smartest man in the 117th Foot. We were in India then, in cantonments, at a place we'll call Bhurtee. Barclay, who died the other day, was sergeant in the same company as myself, and the belle of the regiment – aye, and the finest girl that ever had the breath of life between her lips – was Nancy Devoy, the daughter of the colour-sergeant. There were two men who loved her, and one whom she loved; and you'll smile when you look at this poor thing huddled before the fire, and hear me say that it was for my good looks that she loved me.

'Well, though I had her heart her father was set upon her marrying Barclay. I was a harum-scarum, reckless lad, and he had had an education, and was already marked for the sword-belt. But the girl held true to me, and it seemed that I would have had her, when the Mutiny broke out, and all Hell was loose in the country.

'We were shut up in Bhurtee, the regiment of us, with half a battery of artillery, a company of Sikhs, and a lot of civilians and women-folk. There were ten thousand rebels round us, and they were as keen as a set of terriers round a rat cage. About the second week of it our water gave out, and it was a question whether we could communicate with General Neill's column, which was moving up country. It was our only chance, for we could not hope to fight our way out with all the women and children, so I volunteered to go out and warn General Neill of our danger. My offer was accepted, and I talked it over with Sergeant Barclay, who was supposed to know the ground better than any other man, and who drew up a route by which I might get through the rebel lines. At ten o'clock the same night I started off upon my journey. There were a thousand lives to save, but it was of only one that I was thinking when I dropped over the wall that night.

'My way ran down a dried-up watercourse, which we hoped would screen me from the enemy's sentries, but as I crept round the corner of it I walked right into six of them, who were crouching down in the dark waiting for me. In an instant I was stunned with a blow, and bound hand and foot. But the real blow was to my heart and not to my head, for as I came to and listened to as much as I could understand of their talk, I heard enough to tell me that my comrade, the very man who had arranged the way I was to take, had betrayed me by means of a native servant into the hands of the enemy.

'Well, there's no need for me to dwell on that part of it. You know now what James Barclay was capable of. Bhurtee was relieved by Neill next day, but the rebels took me away with them in their retreat, and it was many a long year before ever I saw a white face again. I was tortured, and tried to get away, and was captured and tortured again. You can see for yourselves the state in which I was left. Some of them that fled into Nepal took me with them, and then afterwards I was up past Darjeeling. The hill-folk up there murdered the rebels who had me, and I became their slave for a time until I escaped, but instead of going south I had to go north, until I found myself among the Afghans. There I wandered about for many a year, and at last came back to the Punjab, where I lived mostly among the natives, and picked up a living by the conjuring tricks that I had learned. What use was it for me, a wretched cripple, to go back to England, or to make myself known to my old comrades? Even my wish for revenge would not make me do that. I had rather that Nancy and my old pals should think of Harry Wood as having died with a straight back, than see him living and crawling with a stick like a chimpanzee. They never doubted that I was dead, and I meant that they never should. I heard that Barclay had married Nancy, and that he was rapidly rising in the regiment, but even that did not make me speak.

'But when one gets old, one has a longing for home. For years I've been dreaming of the bright green fields and the hedges of England. At last I determined to see them before I died. I saved enough to bring me across, and then I came here where the soldiers are, for I know their ways, and how to amuse them, and so earn enough to keep me.'

'Your narrative is most interesting,' said Sherlock Holmes. 'I have already heard of your meeting with Mrs Barclay and your mutual recognition. You then, as I understand, followed her home and saw through the window an altercation between her husband and her, in which she doubtless cast his conduct to you in his teeth. Your own feelings overcame you, and you ran across the lawn, and broke in upon them.'

'I did, sir, and at the sight of me he looked as I have never seen a man look before, and over he went with his head on the fender. But he was dead before he fell. I read death on his face as plain as I can read that text over the fire. The bare sight of me was like a bullet through his guilty heart.'

'And then?'

'Then Nancy fainted, and I caught up the key of the door from her hand, intending to unlock it and get help. But as I was doing it it seemed to me better to leave it alone and get away, for the thing might look black against me, and anyway my secret would be out if I were taken. In my haste I thrust the key into my pocket, and dropped my stick while I was chasing Teddy, who had run up the curtain. When I got him into his box, from which he had slipped, I was off as fast as I could run.'

'Who's Teddy?' asked Holmes.

The man leaned over and pulled up the front of a kind of hutch in the corner. In an instant out there slipped a beautiful reddish-brown creature, thin, and lithe, with the legs of a stoat, a long thin nose, and a pair of the finest red eyes that ever I saw in an animal's head.

'It's a mongoose!' I cried.

'Well, some call them that, and some call them

ichneumon,' said the man. 'Snake-catcher is what I call them, and Teddy is amazing quick on cobras. I have one here without the fangs, and Teddy catches it every night to please the folk in the canteen. Any other point, sir?'

'Well, we may have to apply to you again if Mrs Barclay should prove to be in serious trouble.'

'In that case, of course, I'd come forward.'

'But if not, there is no object in raking up this scandal against a dead man, foully as he has acted. You have, at least, the satisfaction of knowing that for thirty years of his life his conscience bitterly reproached him for his wicked deed. Ah, there goes Major Murphy on the other side of the street. Good-bye, Wood; I want to learn if anything has happened since yesterday.'

We were in time to overtake the Major before he reached the corner.

'Ah, Holmes,' he said, 'I suppose you have heard that all this fuss has come to nothing?'

'What, then?'

'The inquest is just over. The medical evidence showed conclusively that death was due to apoplexy. You see, it was quite a simple case after all.'

'Oh, remarkably superficial,' said Holmes, smiling. 'Come, Watson, I don't think we shall be wanted in Aldershot any more.'

'There's one thing,' said I, as we walked down to the station; 'if the husband's name was James, and the other was Henry, what was this talk about David?'

'That one word, my dear Watson, should have told me the whole story had I been the ideal reasoner which you are so fond of depicting. It was evidently a term of reproach.'

'Of reproach?'

'Yes, David strayed a little now and then, you know, and on one occasion in the same direction as Sergeant James Barclay. You remember the small affair of Uriah and Bathsheba? My Biblical knowledge is a trifle rusty, I fear, but you will find the story in the first or second of Samuel.'

THE FIVE ORANGE PIPS

When I glance over my notes and records of the Sherlock Holmes cases between the years '82 and '90, I am faced by so many which present strange and interesting features, that it is no easy matter to know which to choose and which to leave. Some, however, have already gained publicity through the papers, and others have not offered a field for those peculiar qualities which my friend possessed in so high a degree, and which it is the object of these papers to illustrate. Some, too, have baffled his analytical skill, and would be, as narratives, beginnings without an ending, while others have been but partially cleared up, and have their explanations founded rather upon conjecture and surmise than on that absolute logical proof which was so dear to him. There is, however, one of these last which was so remarkable in its details and so startling in its results, that I am tempted to give some account of it, in spite of the fact that there are points in connection with it which never have been, and probably never will be, entirely cleared up.

The year '87 furnished us with a long series of

cases of greater or less interest, of which I retain the records. Among my headings under this one twelve months, I find an account of the adventure of the Paradol Chamber, of the Amateur Mendicant Society, who held a luxurious club in the lower vault of a furniture warehouse, of the facts connected with the loss of the British barque *Sophy Anderson*, of the singular adventures of the Grice Patersons in the island of Uffa, and finally of the Camberwell poisoning case. In the latter, as may be remembered, Sherlock Holmes was able, by winding up the dead man's watch, to prove that it had been wound up two hours ago, and that therefore the deceased had gone to bed within that time – a deduction which was of the greatest importance in clearing up the case. All these I may sketch out at some future date, but none of them present such singular features as the strange train of circumstances which I have now taken up my pen to describe.

It was in the latter days of September, and the equinoctial gales had set in with exceptional violence. All day the wind had screamed and the rain had beaten against the windows, so that even here in the heart of great, hand-made London we were forced to raise our minds for the instant from the routine of life, and to recognize the presence of those great elemental forces which shriek at mankind through the bars of his civilization, like untamed beasts in a cage. As evening drew in the storm grew louder and louder, and the wind cried and sobbed like a child in the chimney. Sherlock Holmes sat moodily at one side of the fireplace cross-indexing his records of crime, whilst I at the other was deep in one of Clark Russell's fine sea stories, until the howl of the gale from without seemed to blend with the text, and the splash of the rain to lengthen out into the long swash of the sea waves. My wife was on a visit to her aunt's, and for a few days I was a dweller once more in my old quarters at Baker Street.

'Why,' said I, glancing up at my companion, 'that was surely the bell? Who could come tonight? Some friend of yours, perhaps?'

'Except yourself I have none,' he answered. 'I do not encourage visitors.'

'A client, then?'

'If so, it is a serious case. Nothing less would bring a man out on such a day, and at such an hour. But I take it that it is more likely to be some crony of the landlady's.'

Sherlock Holmes was wrong in his conjecture, however, for there came a step in the passage, and a tapping at the door. He stretched out his long arm to turn the lamp away from himself and towards the vacant chair upon which a newcomer must sit. 'Come in!' said he.

The man who entered was young, some two-and-twenty at the outside, well groomed and trimly clad, with something of refinement and delicacy in his bearing. The streaming umbrella which he held in his hand, and his long shining waterproof told of the fierce weather through which he had come. He looked about him anxiously in the glare of the lamp, and I could see that his face was pale and his eyes heavy, like those of a man who is weighed down with some great anxiety.

'I owe you an apology,' he said, raising his golden pince-nez to his eyes. 'I trust that I am not intruding. I fear that I have brought some traces of the storm and the rain into your snug chamber.'

'Give me your coat and umbrella,' said Holmes. 'They may rest here on the hook, and will be dry presently. You have come up from the south-west, I see.'

'Yes, from Horsham.'

'That clay and chalk mixture which I see upon your toecaps is quite distinctive.'

'I have come for advice.'

'That is easily got.'

'And help.'

'That is not always so easy.'

'I have heard of you, Mr Holmes. I heard from Major Prendergast how you saved him in the Tankerville Club Scandal.'

'Ah, of course. He was wrongfully accused of cheating at cards.'

'He said that you could solve anything.'

'He said too much.'

'That you are never beaten.'

'I have been beaten four times – three times by men and once by a woman.'

'But what is that compared with the number of your successes?'

'It is true that I have been generally successful.'

'Then you may be so with me.'

'I beg that you will draw your chair up to the fire, and favour me with some details as to your case.'

'It is no ordinary one.'

'None of those which come to me are. I am the last court of appeal.'

'And yet I question, sir, whether, in all your experience, you have ever listened to a more mysterious and inexplicable chain of events than those which have happened in my own family.'

'You fill me with interest,' said Holmes. 'Pray give us the essential facts from the commencement, and I can afterwards question you as to those details which seem to me to be most important.'

The young man pulled his chair up, and pushed his wet feet out towards the blaze.

'My name,' said he, 'is John Openshaw, but my own affairs have, so far as I can understand it, little to do with this awful business. It is a hereditary matter, so in order to give you an idea of the facts, I must go back to the commencement of the affair.

'You must know that my grandfather had two sons – my uncle Elias and my father Joseph. My father had a small factory at Coventry, which he enlarged at the time of the invention of bicycling.

He was the patentee of the Openshaw unbreakable tyre, and his business met with such success that he was able to sell it, and to retire upon a handsome competence.

'My uncle Elias emigrated to America when he was a young man, and became a planter in Florida, where he was reported to have done very well. At the time of the war he fought in Jackson's army, and afterwards under Hood, where he rose to be a colonel. When Lee laid down his arms my uncle returned to his plantation, where he remained for three or four years. About 1869 or 1870 he came back to Europe, and took a small estate in Sussex, near Horsham. He had made a very considerable fortune in the States, and his reason for leaving them was his aversion to the negroes, and his dislike of the Republican policy in extending the franchise to them. He was a singular man, fierce and quick-tempered, very foul-mouthed when he was angry, and of a most retiring disposition. During all the years that he lived at Horsham I doubt if ever he set foot in the town. He had a garden and two or three fields round his house, and there he would take his exercise, though very often for weeks on end he would never leave his room. He drank a great deal of brandy, and smoked very heavily, but he would see no society, and did not want any friends, not even his own brother.

'He didn't mind me, in fact he took a fancy to me, for at the time when he saw me first I was a youngster of twelve or so. That would be in the year 1878, after he had been eight or nine years in England. He begged my father to let me live with him, and he was very kind to me in his way. When he was sober he used to be fond of playing backgammon and draughts with me, and he would make me his representative both with the servants and with the tradespeople, so that by the time that I was sixteen I was quite master of the house. I kept all the keys, and could go where I liked and do what I liked, so long as I did not disturb him in his privacy. There was one singular exception, however, for he had a single room, a lumber-room up among the attics, which was invariably locked, and which he would never permit either me or anyone else to enter. With a boy's curiosity I have peeped through the keyhole, but I was never able to see more than such a collection of old trunks and bundles as would be expected in such a room.

'One day – it was in March, 1883 – a letter with a foreign stamp lay upon the table in front of the Colonel's plate. It was not a common thing for him to receive letters, for his bills were all paid in ready money, and he had no friends of any sort. "From India!" said he, as he took it up, "Pondicherry postmark! What can this be?" Opening it hurriedly, out there jumped five little dried orange pips, which pattered down upon his plate. I began to laugh at this, but the laugh was struck from my lips at the sight of his face. His lip had fallen, his eyes were protruding, his skin the colour of putty, and he glared at the envelope which he still held in his trembling hand. "K.K.K.," he shrieked, and then: "My God, my God, my sins have overtaken me."

'"What is it, uncle!" I cried.

'"Death," said he, and rising from the table he retired to his room, leaving me palpitating with horror. I took up the envelope, and saw scrawled in red ink upon the inner flap, just above the gum, the letter K three times repeated. There was nothing else save the five dried pips. What could be the reason of his over-powering terror? I left the breakfast-table, and as I ascended the stairs I met him coming down with an old rusty key, which must have belonged to the attic, in one hand, and a small brass box, like a cash box, in the other.

'"They may do what they like, but I'll checkmate them still," said he, with an oath. "Tell Mary that I shall want a fire in my room today, and send down to Fordham, the Horsham lawyer."

'I did as he ordered, and when the lawyer arrived I was asked to step up to the room. The fire was burning brightly, and in the grate there was a mass of black, fluffy ashes, as of burned paper, while the brass box stood open and empty beside it. As I glanced at the box I noticed, with a start, that upon the lid were printed the treble K which I had read in the morning upon the envelope.

'"I wish you, John," said my uncle, "to witness

my will. I leave my estate, with all its advantages
and all its disadvantages to my brother, your
father, whence it will, no doubt, descend to you.
If you can enjoy it in peace, well and good! If you
find you cannot, take my advice, my boy, and
leave it to your deadliest enemy. I am sorry to
give you such a two-edged thing, but I can't say
what turn things are going to take. Kindly sign
the paper where Mr Fordham shows you."

'I signed the paper as directed, and the lawyer
took it away with him. The singular incident
made, as you may think, the deepest impression
upon me, and I pondered over it, and turned it
every way in my mind without being able to make
anything of it. Yet I could not shake off the vague
feeling of dread which it left behind it, though the
sensation grew less keen as the weeks passed, and
nothing happened to disturb the usual routine of
our lives. I could see a change in my uncle, however. He drank more than ever, and he was less
inclined for any sort of society. Most of his time
he would spend in his room, with the door locked
upon the inside, but sometimes he would emerge
in a sort of drunken frenzy and would burst out of
the house and tear about the garden with a revolver in his hand, screaming out that he was
afraid of no man, and that he was not to be
cooped up, like a sheep in a pen, by man or devil.
When these hot fits were over, however, he would
rush tumultuously in at the door, and lock and
bar it behind him, like a man who can brazen it

out no longer against the terror which lies at the roots of his soul. At such times I have seen his face even on a cold day, glisten with moisture as though it were new raised from a basin.

'Well, to come to an end of the matter, Mr Holmes, and not to abuse your patience, there came a night when he made one of those drunken sallies from which he never came back. We found him, when we went to search for him, face downwards in a little green-scummed pool, which lay at the foot of the garden. There was no sign of any violence, and the water was but two feet deep, so that the jury, having regard to his known eccentricity, brought in a verdict of suicide. But I, who knew how he winced from the very thought of death, had much ado to persuade myself that he had gone out of his way to meet it. The matter passed, however, and my father entered into possession of the estate, and of some fourteen thousand pounds, which lay to his credit at the bank.'

'One moment,' Holmes interposed. 'Your statement is, I foresee, one of the most remarkable to which I have ever listened. Let me have the date of the reception by your uncle of the letter, and the date of his supposed suicide.'

'The letter arrived on March the 10th, 1883. His death was seven weeks later, upon the night of the 2nd of May.'

'Thank you. Pray proceed.'

'When my father took over the Horsham property, he, at my request, made a careful examination

THE FIVE ORANGE PIPS 227

of the attic, which had been always locked up. We found the brass box there, although its contents had been destroyed. On the inside of the cover was a paper label, with the initials K. K. K. repeated upon it, and "Letters, memoranda, receipts and a register" written beneath. These, we presume, indicated the nature of the papers which had been destroyed by Colonel Openshaw. For the rest, there was nothing of much importance in the attic, save a great many scattered papers and notebooks bearing upon my uncle's life in America. Some of them were of the war time, and showed that he had done his duty well, and had borne the repute of being a brave soldier. Others were of a date during the reconstruction of the Southern States, and were mostly concerned with politics for he had evidently taken a strong part in opposing the carpet-bag politicians who had been sent down from the North.

'Well, it was the beginning of '84, when my father came to live at Horsham, and all went as well as possible with us until the January of '85. On the fourth day after the New Year I heard my father give a sharp cry of surprise as we sat together at the breakfast-table. There he was, sitting with a newly opened envelope in one hand and five dried orange pips in the outstretched palm of the other one. He had always laughed at what he called my cock-and-bull story about the Colonel, but he looked very puzzled and scared now that the same thing had come upon himself.

'"Why, what on earth does this mean, John?" he stammered.

'My heart had turned to lead. "It is K. K. K.," said I.

'He looked inside the envelope. "So it is," he cried. "Here are the very letters. But what is this written above them?"

'"Put the papers on the sundial," I read, peeping over his shoulder.

'"What papers? What sundial?" he asked.

'"The sundial in the garden. There is no other," said I; "but the papers must be those that are destroyed."

'"Pooh!" said he, gripping hard at his courage. "We are in a civilized land here, and we can't have tomfoolery of this kind. Where does the thing come from?"

'"From Dundee," I answered, glancing at the postmark.

'"Some preposterous practical joke," said he. "What have I to do with sundials and papers? I shall take no notice of such nonsense."

'"I should certainly speak to the police," I said.

'"And be laughed at for my pains. Nothing of the sort."

'"Then let me do so."

'"No, I forbid you. I won't have a fuss made over such nonsense."

'It was in vain to argue with him, for he was a very obstinate man. I went about, however, with a heart which was full of forebodings.

'On the third day after the coming of the letter my father went from home to visit an old friend of his, Major Freebody, who is in command of one of the forts upon Portsdown Hill. I was glad that he should go, for it seemed to me that he was farther from danger when he was away from home. In that, however, I was in error. Upon the second day of his absence I received a telegram from the Major, imploring me to come at once. My father had fallen over one of the deep chalk-pits which abound in the neighbourhood, and was lying sense-less, with a shattered skull. I hurried to him, but he passed away without having ever recovered his consciousness. He had, as it appears, been return-ing from Fareham in the twilight, and as the country was unknown to him, and the chalk-pit unfenced, the jury had no hesitation in bringing in a verdict of "Death from accidental causes". Carefully as I examined every fact connected with his death, I was unable to find anything which could suggest the idea of murder. There were no signs of violence, no footmarks, no robbery, no record of strangers having been seen upon the roads. And yet I need not tell you that my mind was far from at ease, and that I was wellnigh certain that some foul plot had been woven round him.

'In this sinister way I came into my inheritance. You will ask me why I did not dispose of it? I answer because I was well convinced that our troubles were in some way dependent upon an incident in my uncle's life, and that the danger would be as pressing in one house as in another.

'It was in January, '85, that my poor father met his end, and two years and eight months have elapsed since then. During that time I have lived happily at Horsham, and I had begun to hope that this curse had passed away from the family, and that it had ended with the last generation. I had begun to take comfort too soon, however; yesterday morning the blow fell in the very shape in which it had come upon my father.'

The young man took from his waistcoat a crumpled envelope, and, turning to the table, he shook out upon it five little dried orange pips.

'This is the envelope,' he continued. 'The postmark is London – eastern division. Within are the very words which were upon my father's last message. "K. K. K."; and then "Put the papers on the sundial".'

'What have you done?' asked Holmes.

'Nothing.'

'Nothing?'

'To tell the truth' – he sank his face into his thin, white hands – 'I have felt helpless. I have felt like one of those poor rabbits when the snake is writhing towards it. I seem to be in the grasp of some resistless, inexorable evil, which no foresight and no precautions can guard against.'

'Tut! Tut!' cried Sherlock Holmes. 'You must act, man, or you are lost. Nothing but energy can save you. This is no time for despair.'

'I have seen the police.'

'Ah?'

'But they listened to my story with a smile. I am convinced that the inspector has formed the opinion that the letters are all practical jokes, and that the deaths of my relations were really accidents, as the jury stated, and were not to be connected with the warnings.'

Holmes shook his clenched hands in the air. 'Incredible imbecility!' he cried.

'They have, however, allowed me a policeman, who may remain in the house with me.'

'Has he come with you tonight?'

'No. His orders were to stay in the house.'

Again Holmes raved in the air.

'Why did you come to me?' he said; 'and, above all, why did you not come at once?'

'I did not know. It was only today that I spoke to Major Prendergast about my trouble, and was advised by him to come to you.'

'It is really two days since you had the letter. We should have acted before this. You have no further evidence, I suppose, than that which you have placed before us – no suggestive detail which might help us?'

'There is one thing,' said John Openshaw. He rummaged in his coat pocket, and drawing out a piece of discoloured, blue-tinted paper, he laid it out upon the table. 'I have some remembrance,' said he, 'that on the day when my uncle burned the papers I observed that the small, unburned margins which lay amid the ashes were of this particular colour. I found this single sheet upon the floor of his room, and I am inclined to think that it may be one of the papers which had, perhaps, fluttered out from among the others, and in that way escaped destruction. Beyond the mention of pips, I do not see that it helps us much. I think myself that it is a page from some private diary. The writing is undoubtedly my uncle's.'

Holmes moved the lamp, and we both bent over the sheet of paper, which showed by its ragged edge that it had indeed been torn from a book. It was headed 'March, 1869', and beneath were the following enigmatical notices:

4th. Hudson came. Same old platform.
7th. Set the pips on McCauley, Paramore, and John Swain of St Augustine.
9th. McCauley cleared.
10th. John Swain cleared.
12th. Visited Paramore. All well.

'Thank you!' said Holmes, folding up the paper and returning it to our visitor. 'And now you must on no account lose another instant. We cannot spare time even to discuss what you have told me. You must get home instantly, and act.'

'What shall I do?'

'There is but one thing to do. It must be done at once. You must put this piece of paper which you have shown us into the brass box which you have described. You must also put in a note to say that all the other papers were burned by your uncle, and that this is the only one which remains. You must assert that in such words as will carry conviction with them. Having done this, you must at once put the box out upon the sundial, as directed. Do you understand?'

'Entirely.'

'Do not think of revenge, or anything of the sort, at present. I think that we may gain that by means of the law; but we have our web to weave, while theirs is already woven. The first consideration is to remove the pressing danger which threatens you. The second is to clear up the mystery, and to punish the guilty parties.'

'I thank you,' said the young man, rising, and pulling on his overcoat. 'You have given me fresh life and hope. I shall certainly do as you advise.'

'Do not lose an instant. And, above all, take care of yourself in the meanwhile, for I do not think that there can be a doubt that you are threatened by a very real and imminent danger. How do you go back?'

'By train from Waterloo.'

'It is not yet nine. The streets will be crowded, so I trust that you may be in safety. And yet you cannot guard yourself too closely.'

'I am armed.'

'That is well. Tomorrow I shall set to work upon your case.'

'I shall see you at Horsham, then?'

'No, your secret lies in London. It is there that I shall seek it.'

'Then I shall call upon you in a day, or in two days, with news as to the box and the papers. I shall take your advice in every particular.' He shook hands with us, and took his leave. Outside the wind still screamed, and the rain splashed and pattered against the windows. This strange, wild story seemed to have come to us from amid the mad elements – blown in upon us like a sheet of seaweed in a gale – and now to have been re-absorbed by them once more.

Sherlock Holmes sat for some time in silence with his head sunk forward, and his eyes bent upon the red glow of the fire. Then he lit his pipe, and leaning back in his chair he watched the blue smoke rings as they chased each other up to the ceiling.

'I think, Watson,' he remarked at last, 'that of all our cases we have had none more fantastic than this.'

'Save, perhaps, the Sign of Four.'

'Well, yes. Save, perhaps, that. And yet this John Openshaw seems to me to be walking amid even greater perils than did the Sholtos.'

'But have you,' I asked, 'formed any definite conception as to what these perils are?'

'There can be no question as to their nature,' he answered.

'Then what are they? Who is this K. K. K., and why does he pursue this unhappy family?'

Sherlock Holmes closed his eyes, and placed his elbows upon the arms of his chair, with his fingertips together. 'The ideal reasoner,' he remarked, 'would, when he has once been shown a single fact in all its bearings, deduce from it not only all the chain of events which led up to it, but also all the results which would follow from it. As Cuvier could correctly describe a whole animal by the contemplation of a single bone, so the observer who has thoroughly understood one link in a series of incidents, should be able accurately to state all the other ones, both before and after. We have not yet grasped the results which the reason alone can attain to. Problems may be solved in the study which have baffled all those who have sought a solution by the aid of their senses. To carry the art, however, to its highest pitch, it is necessary that the reasoner should be able to utilize all the facts which have come to his knowledge, and this in itself implies, as you will readily see, a possession of all knowledge, which, even in these days of free education and encyclopedias, is a somewhat rare accomplishment. It is not so impossible, however, that a man should possess all knowledge which is likely to be useful to him in his work, and this I have endeavoured in my case to do. If I remember rightly, you on one occasion, in the early days of our friendship, defined my limits in a very precise fashion.'

'Yes,' I answered, laughing. 'It was a singular

document. Philosophy, astronomy, and politics were marked at zero, I remember. Botany variable, geology profound as regards the mudstains from any region within fifty miles of town, chemistry eccentric, anatomy unsystematic, sensational literature and crime records unique, violin player, boxer, swordsman, lawyer, and self-poisoner by cocaine and tobacco. Those, I think, were the main points of my analysis.'

Holmes grinned at the last item. 'Well,' he said, 'I say now, as I said then, that a man should keep his little brain attic stocked with all the furniture that he is likely to use, and the rest he can put away in the lumber-room of his library, where he can get it if he wants it. Now, for such a case as the one which has been submitted to us tonight, we need certainly to muster all our resources. Kindly hand me down the letter K of the American Encyclopedia which stands upon the shelf beside you. Thank you. Now let us consider the situation, and see what may be deduced from it. In the first place, we may start with a strong presumption that Colonel Openshaw had some very strong reason for leaving America. Men at his time of life do not change all their habits, and exchange willingly the charming climate of Florida for the lonely life of an English provincial town. His extreme love of solitude in England suggests the idea that he was in fear of someone or something, which drove him from America. As to what it was he feared, we can only deduce that by

considering the formidable letters which were received by himself and his successors. Did you
remark the postmarks of those letters?'

'The first was from Pondicherry, the second
from Dundee, and the third from London.'

'From East London. What do you deduce from
that?'

'They are all seaports. That the writer was on
board a ship.'

'Excellent. We have already a clue. There can
be no doubt that the probability – the strong
probability – is that the writer was on board of a
ship. And now let us consider another point. In
the case of Pondicherry seven weeks elasped between the threat and its fulfilment, in Dundee it
was only some three or four days. Does that suggest anything?'

'A greater distance to travel.'

'But the letter had also a greater distance to
come.'

'Then I do not see the point.'

'There is at least a presumption that the vessel
in which the man or men are is a sailing ship. It
looks as if they always sent their singular warning
or token before them when starting upon their
mission. You see how quickly the deed followed
the sign when it came from Dundee. If they had
come from Pondicherry in a steamer they would
have arrived almost as soon as their letter. But as
a matter of fact seven weeks elapsed. I think that
those seven weeks represented the difference

between the mail boat which brought the letter, and the sailing vessel which brought the writer.'

'It is possible.'

'More than that. It is probable. And now you see the deadly urgency of this new case, and why I urged young Openshaw to caution. The blow has always fallen at the end of the time which it would take the senders to travel the distance. But this one comes from London, and therefore we cannot count upon delay.'

'Good God!' I cried. 'What can it mean, this relentless persecution?'

'The papers which Openshaw carried are obviously of vital importance to the person or persons in the sailing ship. I think that it is quite clear that there must be more than one of them. A single man could not have carried out two deaths in such a way as to deceive a coroner's jury. There must have been several in it, and they must have been men of resource and determination. Their papers they mean to have, be the holder of them who it may. In this way you see K. K. K. ceases to be the initials of an individual, and becomes the badge of a society.'

'But of what society?'

'Have you never –' said Sherlock Holmes, bending forward and sinking his voice – 'have you never heard of the Ku Klux Klan?'

'I never have.'

Holmes turned over the leaves of the book upon his knee. 'Here it is,' said he presently, '"Ku

Klux Klan. A name derived from a fanciful resemblance to the sound produced by cocking a rifle. This terrible secret society was formed by some ex-Confederate soldiers in the Southern States after the Civil War, and it rapidly formed local branches in different parts of the country, notably in Tennessee, Louisiana, the Carolinas, Georgia, and Florida. Its power was used for political purposes, principally for the terrorizing of the negro voters, and the murdering or driving from the country of those who were opposed to its views. Its outrages were usually preceded by a warning sent to the marked man in some fantastic but generally recognized shape – a sprig of oak leaves in some parts, melon seeds or orange pips in others. On receiving this the victim might either openly abjure his former ways, or might fly from the country. If he braved the matter out, death would unfailingly come upon him, and usually in some strange and unforeseen manner. So perfect was the organization of the society, and so systematic its methods, that there is hardly a case upon record where any man succeeded in braving it with impunity, or in which any of its outrages were traced home to the perpetrators. For some years the organization flourished, in spite of the efforts of the United States Government, and of the better classes of the community in the South. Eventually, in the year 1869, the movement rather suddenly collapsed, although there have been sporadic outbreaks of the same sort since that date.''

'You will observe,' said Holmes, laying down the volume, 'that the sudden breaking up of the society was coincident with the disappearance of Openshaw from America with their papers. It may well have been cause and effect. It is no wonder that he and his family have some of the more implacable spirits upon their track. You can understand that this register and diary may implicate some of the first men in the South, and that there may be many who will not sleep easy at night until it is recovered.'

'Then the page which we have seen –'

'Is such as we might expect. It ran, if I remember right, "sent the pips to A, B, and C" – that is, sent the society's warning to them. Then there are successive entries that A and B cleared, or left the country, and finally that C was visited, with, I fear, a sinister result for C. Well, I think, Doctor, that we may let some light into this dark place, and I believe that the only chance young Openshaw has in the meantime is to do what I have told him. There is nothing more to be said or to be done tonight, so hand me over my violin and let us try to forget for half an hour the miserable weather, and the still more miserable ways of our fellow-men.'

It had cleared in the morning, and the sun was shining with a subdued brightness through the dim veil which hangs over the great city. Sherlock Holmes was already at breakfast when I came down.

'You will excuse me for not waiting for you,' said he; 'I have, I forsee, a very busy day before me in looking into this case of young Openshaw's.'

'What steps will you take?' I asked.

'It will very much depend upon the results of my first inquiries. I may have to go down to Horsham after all.'

'You will not go there first?'

'No, I shall commence with the City. Just ring the bell, and the maid will bring up your coffee.'

As I waited, I lifted the unopened newspaper from the table and glanced my eye over it. It rested upon a heading which sent a chill to my heart.

'Holmes,' I cried, 'you are too late.'

'Ah!' said he, laying down his cup, 'I feared as much. How was it done?' He spoke calmly, but I could see that he was deeply moved.

'My eye caught the name of Openshaw, and the heading "Tragedy near Waterloo Bridge". Here is the account: "Between nine and ten last night Police Constable Cook, of the H Division, on duty near Waterloo Bridge, heard a cry for help and a splash in the water. The night, however, was extremely dark and stormy, so that, in spite of the help of several passers-by, it was quite impossible to effect a rescue. The alarm, however, was given, and by the aid of the water police, thc body was eventually recovered. It proved to be that of a young gentleman whose name, as it appears from an envelope which was found in his pocket, was John Openshaw, and whose residence is near Horsham. It is conjectured that he may have been hurrying down to catch the last train from Waterloo station, and that in his haste and the extreme darkness, he missed his path and walked over the edge of one of the small landing-places for river steamboats. The body exhibited no traces of violence, and there can be no doubt that the deceased had been the victim of an unfortunate accident, which should have the effect of calling the attention of the authorities to the condition of the riverside landing-stages."'

We sat in silence for some minutes, Holmes more depressed and shaken than I had ever seen him.

'That hurts my pride, Watson,' he said at last. 'It is a petty feeling, no doubt, but it hurts my pride. It becomes a personal matter with me now, and, if God sends me health, I shall set my hand upon this gang. That he should come to me for help, and that I should send him away to his death –!' He sprang from his chair, and paced about the room in uncontrollable agitation, with a flush upon his sallow cheeks, and a nervous clasping and unclasping of his long, thin hands.

'They must be cunning devils,' he exclaimed at last. 'How could they have decoyed him down there? The Embankment is not on the direct line to the station. The bridge, no doubt, was too crowded, even on such a night, for their purpose.

Well, Watson, we shall see who will win in the long run. I am going out now!'

'To the police?'

'No; I shall be my own police. When I have spun the web they may take the flies, but not before.'

All day I was engaged in my professional work, and it was late in the evening before I returned to Baker Street. Sherlock Holmes had not come back yet. It was nearly ten o'clock before he entered, looking pale and worn. He walked up to the sideboard, and, tearing a piece from the loaf, he devoured it voraciously, washing it down with a long draught of water.

'You are hungry,' I remarked.

'Starving. It had escaped my memory. I have had nothing since breakfast.'

'Nothing?'

'Not a bite. I had no time to think of it.'

'And how have you succeeded?'

'Well.'

'You have a clue?'

'I have them in the hollow of my hand. Young Openshaw shall not remain long unavenged. Why, Watson, let us put their own devilish trade-mark upon them. It is well thought of!'

'What do you mean?'

He took an orange from the cupboard, and tearing it to pieces, he squeezed out the pips upon the table. Of these he took five, and thrust them into an envelope. On the inside of the flap he wrote, 'S.H. for J.O.' Then he sealed it and addressed it to 'Captain James Calhoun, Barque *Lone Star*, Savannah, Georgia'.

'That will await him when he enters port,' said he, chuckling. 'It may give him a sleepless night. He will find it as sure a precursor of his fate as Openshaw did before him.'

'And who is this Captain Calhoun?'

'The leader of the gang. I shall have the others, but he first.'

'How did you trace it, then?'

He took a large sheet of paper from his pockets, all covered with dates and names.

'I have spent the whole day,' said he, 'over Lloyd's registers and the files of old papers, following the future career of every vessel which touched at Pondicherry in January and in February in '83. There were thirty-six ships of fair tonnage which were reported there during those months. Of these, the *Lone Star* instantly attracted my attention, since, although it was reported as having cleared from London, the name is that which is given to one of the States of the Union.'

'Texas, I think.'

'I was not and am not sure which; but I knew that the ship must have an American origin.'

'What then?'

'I searched the Dundee records, and when I found that the barque *Lone Star* was there in January, '85, my suspicion became a certainty. I then inquired as to vessels which lay at present in the port of London.'

'Yes?'

'The *Lone Star* had arrived here last week. I went down to the Albert dock, and found that she had been taken down the river by the early tide this morning, homeward bound to Savannah. I wired to Gravesend, and learned that she had passed some time ago, and as the wind is easterly, I have no doubt that she is now past the Goodwins, and not very far from the Isle of Wight.'

'What will you do, then?'

'Oh, I have my hand upon him. He and the two mates are, as I learn, the only native-born Americans in the ship. The others are Finns and Germans. I also know that they were all three away from the ship last night. I had it from the stevedore, who has been loading their cargo. By the time their sailing ship reaches Savannah the mail boat will have carried this letter, and the cable will have informed the police of Savannah that these three gentlemen are badly wanted here upon a charge of murder.'

There is ever a flaw, however, in the best laid of human plans, and the murderers of John Openshaw were never to receive the orange pips which would show them that another, as cunning and resolute as themselves, was upon their track. Very long and severe were the equinoctial gales of that year. We waited long for news of the *Lone Star* of Savannah, but none ever reached us. We did at last hear that somewhere far out in the Atlantic a shattered sternpost of a boat was seen swinging in the trough of a wave, with the letters 'L.S.' carved upon it, and that is all which we shall ever know of the fate of the *Lone Star*.

THE GREAT ADVENTURES OF SHERLOCK HOLMES
Sir Arthur Conan Doyle

From the strange case of The Red-Headed League to the extraordinary tale of The Engineer's Thumb, Sherlock Holmes and his assistant Dr Watson grapple with treachery, murder, and ingenious crimes of all kinds. But no case is too challenging, no mystery unsolvable, for the immortal detective's unique powers of deduction.

THE HOUND OF THE BASKERVILLES
Sir Arthur Conan Doyle

When Sir Charles Baskerville is found mysteriously dead in the grounds of Baskerville Hall, everyone remembers the legend of the monstrous creature that haunts the moor. The greatest detective in the world, Sherlock Holmes knows there must be a more rational explanation – but the difficulty is to find it before the hellhound finds him . . .

READ MORE IN PUFFIN

For children of all ages, Puffin represents quality and variety – the very best in publishing today around the world.

For complete information about books available from Puffin – and Penguin – and how to order them, contact us at the appropriate address below. Please note that for copyright reasons the selection of books varies from country to country.

On the worldwide web: www.puffin.co.uk

In the United Kingdom: Please write to *Dept. EP, Penguin Books Ltd, Bath Road, Harmondsworth, West Drayton, Middlesex UB7 0DA*

In the United States: Please write to *Consumer Sales, Penguin USA, P.O. Box 999, Dept. 17109, Bergenfield, New Jersey 07621-0120.* VISA and MasterCard holders call 1-800-253-6476 to order Penguin titles

In Canada: Please write to *Penguin Books Canada Ltd, 10 Alcorn Avenue, Suite 300, Toronto, Ontario M4V 3B2*

In Australia: Please write to *Penguin Books Australia Ltd, P.O. Box 257, Ringwood, Victoria 3134*

In New Zealand: Please write to *Penguin Books (NZ) Ltd, Private Bag 102902, North Shore Mail Centre, Auckland 10*

In India: Please write to *Penguin Books India Pvt Ltd, 706 Eros Apartments, 56 Nehru Place, New Delhi 110 019*

In the Netherlands: Please write to *Penguin Books Netherlands bv, Postbus 3507, NL-1001 AH Amsterdam*

In Germany: Please write to *Penguin Books Deutschland GmbH, Metzlerstrasse 26, 60594 Frankfurt am Main*

In Spain: Please write to *Penguin Books S. A., Bravo Murillo 19, 1° B, 28015 Madrid*

In Italy: Please write to *Penguin Italia s.r.l., Via Felice Casati 20, I–20124 Milano.*

In France: Please write to *Penguin France S. A., 17 rue Lejeune, F–31000 Toulouse*

In Japan: Please write to *Penguin Books Japan, Ishikiribashi Building, 2–5–4, Suido, Bunkyo-ku, Tokyo 112*

In South Africa: Please write to *Longman Penguin Southern Africa (Pty) Ltd, Private Bag X08, Bertsham 2013*